Aeris Legends 3:
The Lady's Grace
A Prequel to Redeemer Chronicles

By Julie C. Gilbert

Aletheia Pyralis Publishers

http://www.juliecgilbert.com/
https://sites.google.com/view/juliecgilbert-writer/

Love Science Fiction or Mystery?
Choose your adventure!

Visit: http://www.juliecgilbert.com/

For details on getting free ebooks.

Dedication:

To Rachel Rossano. Thanks for the awesome covers.

Note to the Reader: You may want to read *River's Edge Ransom, The Huntsman and the Healer,* and *The Dark Man's Wrath* first. This is book 3 in a very closely linked trilogy.

If you wish to jump right in, check out: What's Gone on Before.

Aeris maps available upon request, please email Devyaschildren@gmail.com

Table of Contents:

Who's Who and What's What:

Aeris – a planet created by Kailon

People Types:
Saroth – A people who live on the east side of Aeris's main continent. They are usually Gifted in the darker four of the seven magic schools and tend to become Destroyers, Shapeshifters, Conjurers, or Minders.
Arkonai – A people who live mainly in the northwest corner of Aeris's main continent. They are usually Gifted in the lighter three of the seven magic schools and tend to become Seekers, Guardians, or Healers.
Bereft – Majority of people on Aeris who have no access to magic.

Key Saroth:
Marina Castaloni-Saveron – Vic's recently deceased mother, Daniel's wife, Corabelle's daughter
Jackson Castaloni – Conjurer, younger brother to Marina, older brother to Gabriel
Gabriel Castaloni – Shapeshifter (squirrel, wolf, beetle), younger brother to Jackson and Marina, engaged to Tielle
Tielle Toscano – Conjurer, engaged to Gabriel
Corabelle Castaloni – Conjurer, Marina's mother, member of the Tariku League
Marcus Polani – Minder, Katrina's father
Katrina Polani – Shapeshifter, Vic's friend

Key Arkonai:
Daniel Saveron – Huntsman, Seeker, Marina's husband, Vic's father
Raelyn Cordova – Healer, Marina's apprentice
Christa Lekros – friend to Daniel and Marina, Healer, Jordan's wife
Jordan Lekros – Daniel's friend, Christa's Husband, Supreme Huntmaster
Shadow – son of Christa and Jordan, Vic's friend
Tellen – son of Callen and Ireena, Vic's friend

Other:
Kailon – Eternal King, Creator of Aeris
The Lady – immortal servant of Kailon
Dark Man – Jackson's master, a manifestation of the Outcast, an immortal who rebelled against Kailon

Key Locations: (maps available upon request)
Caramore – section of Aeris's main continent controlled by Saroth
Bastion – Arkonai capital city; seat of the High Council
Dominance – Saroth capital city; seat of the Tariku League
Aridel – Arkonai; located on the northwest side of Aeris's main continent
Temperance – neutral city; located in the center of Aeris's main continent
Outreach – neutral city; located on the southeast side of Aeris's main continent
River's Edge – Bereft village on the southwest side of Aeris's main continent; site of an old controversy surrounding Marina

What's Gone on Before?
Warning, contains spoilers for the works mentioned

In *River's Edge Ransom*, Jackson Castaloni forces his younger brother, Gabriel, to help him release a deadly disease upon the village of River's Edge. Next, he disguises himself as an Arkonai Huntmaster to hire Huntsman Seeker Daniel Saveron to kill his sister. Once Daniel discovers that Marina Castaloni is trying to save the villagers, he breaks his contract and helps her. Jackson promises Marina the cure in exchange for the sign of her birthright and her Destroyer Gifts. She pays the ransom, but Jackson tries to kill her anyway. Gabriel and Daniel fight Jackson. Gabriel's gravely wounded, but Marina uses some of her life energy and Daniel's to save her brother.

The Huntsman and the Healer picks up right after *River's Edge Ransom* and covers the odd courtship between Marina and Daniel. He fulfills a promise to Marina by escorting her to the Arkonai city of Aridel. When he returns to Bastion to explain himself, the High Council contracts Daniel to capture Marina for questioning in the River's Edge affair. To spare Marina the discomfort of prison, Daniel and his friend, Christa Arrington, make the arrest and move her to Christa's estate.

A cruel trick brings Marina out into the open where Christa's uncle, the Supreme Huntmaster, arrests her. Marina spends several months in prison. Daniel visits often and questions her about Saroth life. Within the stark prison walls, their friendship deepens into genuine affection. A twist of fate has them fleeing the prison. They seek and receive a blessing from Marina's father shortly before his death. Their union is formalized by exchanging marriage vows at the Alamon Temple.

The Dark Man's Wrath begins with the wedding of Marcus Polani and Gabriella Castaloni (formerly Ricci). Marina finally agrees to run the Castaloni family businesses, even though her true passion lies in charity work. Marcus and Daniel join their Gifts to investigate various crimes, including the theft of funds from the Arkonai Hunting Guild's treasury.

Several relatively peaceful years pass. Marina takes on an apprentice, Raelyn. Marcus and Gabriella have a daughter named Katrina. Then, the investigation turns dangerous. Arkonai Brotherhood men capture Marina and force Daniel and Marcus to surrender. Jackson is integral in saving their lives and recovering the money. Soon thereafter, Marina discovers she's pregnant. In the due course of time, she and Daniel have a daughter, Victoria.

The Dark Man wants Daniel to retrieve something for him. To get to him, he must first kill Gabriella. The first phase goes well, but once drawn into a new trap, Marina sacrifices herself for her daughter and her apprentice. Vic is wounded. The Dark Man tells Daniel about a pair of magic bracers that can save Victoria.

Prologue:
Pure Instinct

Home of Daniel and Marina, City of Outreach
The night of Marina's death
(Vic is eight months old)

Daniel Saveron can't feel anything. He's alone despite the crowd milling about inside his home. He doesn't know who Raelyn Cordova called, but she must have reached a Minder because word spread quickly. First, Marina's brother, Gabriel, arrived with his fiancée. Next, her mother, Corabelle Castaloni, appeared. After that, Daniel lost track of the order of arrivals, though he's grateful for their presence. Marcus Polani holds his daughter, Katrina, and speaks with Mika Forester, counselor and purser for Marina's house. Callen and his family huddle in the kitchen area looking ill at ease. Somebody must have contacted both the Arkonai High Council and the Tariku League as well as the Outreach City Council because representatives from each mill about uneasily.

Strange gathering. Marina would approve.

The thought brings pain, but it's muted by weariness. Daniel's eyes flit over the crowd. The officials occupy opposite corners holding cups of something, speaking quietly with their entourages, and studiously ignoring each other.

Some things don't change.

Daniel has already answered more questions than he cares to, yet he understands many more await him. Truthfully, he'd love the answer to many questions posed to him this night. How did Marina die? The dagger wound stands out as the obvious answer, but Raelyn claims there's no evidence for poison. Furthermore, the blood loss alone

1

shouldn't have been enough. The Dark Man had helped Daniel transfer enough lifeforce to let Marina survive the teleportation home. But how did she come to that weakened state in the first place? What other circumstances led to her death? He'd found her in the Earth Temple Ruins, west of Outreach. She couldn't have gotten there without a Teleportation scroll, but he'd used their only one a few days ago to get to Bleakwood Forest. Marina could have obtained another, but aside from rarely exerting the privilege of using the expensive scrolls, why would she go to the Earth Temple with their daughter?

As with Victoria's birth, food covers every flat surface despite the late hour. Daniel desperately wishes this were that happy occasion.

The wish fails.

Reality remains.

Marina's gone.

Her body lies in the next room, lovingly laid atop the bed and covered with a blanket. Raelyn had helped him with that task. Part of Daniel would prefer spending the night clutching Marina's cold hand, privately mourning her death. He would have been content to leave the body leaning against the bed, but his wife deserved better. He'd failed to protect her in life, but he would see her honored in death.

Muffled sobs seep through the closed bedroom door and fill the tiny home. Daniel's instincts to fix problems and seek out answers run hard into helplessness. He wants to comfort Marina's mother, but he doesn't know how. The best he can do is let Raelyn keep people out of the room, so Corabelle and Gabriel can say farewell in their own way. He had some alone time earlier before the guests arrived, and they would eventually leave. What happens next will depend on the conversation yet to happen between him and Marina's immediate family. His gut clenches. He doesn't know much about Saroth funerals, other than that they involve fire, but he's going to have to learn quickly.

Many of his people will criticize the choice to let Marina's family conduct a Saroth funeral. Whether they speak to him or not, they'll grumble that proper respect for the dead demands immediate burial. Daniel intends to bury his beloved near the cabin he'd built for them in the Karnok Mountains.

She never even saw it.

For some reason, the realization strikes Daniel hard, making the previous worries over her reaction to the getaway cabin seem ridiculous.

We never even got to argue about my demotion.

Supreme Huntmaster Jordan Lekros had sacrificed Daniel's

teaching position in Bastion for a few extra votes to get some renovations to Fort Faith approved. Huntmaster Pine and Jordan didn't even have the grace to hide it well. They claimed the move revolved around Daniel being a highly skilled Seeker, but really, it had to do with blatant prejudice. The implication being that the demotion had to do with Marina.

She would have laughed, shaken her head, and shrugged at that.

A hush falls over the crowded room, slowly penetrating Daniel's dazed state.

Attention fixes on the room's center where somebody had turned a large fruit basket into a makeshift bed for Vic. She's crying. Huntsman Callen's son, Tellen, sits beside the basket, gently rocking it back and forth. Marcus Polani's daughter, Katrina, sits on the basket's other side, holding her knees and rocking.

Wearily, Daniel hauls himself off the couch, intending to comfort his daughter.

Marcus catches his arm.

"Wait," he says.

"What's happening?" calls Huntmaster Winston.

Several people gesture for patience and silence.

"Transformation magic is gathering," Tielle explains.

"How do you know that?" demands Elder Loran.

"There's a shift in the magic currents," says Tielle. "Watch the girl." She waves to Katrina Polani.

Vic continues crying.

Tellen abandons his post by the basket and runs to his mother. Lady Ireena picks up her son and changes position so he can continue watching the basket.

Katrina gets up and sits down again. She changes position about a dozen times. Looking to her father, she whines long and loud. Midway through, the noise changes pitch, sailing higher. The girl curls into a ball on the floor, then springs back up in a different shape.

Vic stops crying, letting silence fall.

Two barks shatter the stillness.

The Arkonai and Bereft murmur in astonishment.

The Saroth smile or chuckle.

Vic starts fussing again.

"I've never seen such a thing," mutters Elder Loran.

"Congratulations, Marcus," says Tielle. "Your daughter has discovered her second form, and it's adorable."

The black Lab puppy commands everybody's attention. She darts around the room several times, sniffing everything and occasionally barking. Finally, the puppy leaps into the basket, emits a plaintive noise, and flops down beside Vic.

The baby instinctively reaches for the puppy, too fascinated to continue crying.

Tellen squirms enough to gain release from his mother. Dropping to his knees beside the basket, he reaches to pet the puppy.

Several people start speaking, but Marcus silences them.

"It's all right. Let's see what happens."

When the boy's hand drifts close to the puppy's head, she turns enough to lick the hand. Giggling, he gently strokes the fur along her head and back. Then, he curls up with his back pressed against the basket and closes his eyes.

"You shouldn't encourage such behavior," scolds Elder Loran. "It isn't proper."

"It's pure instinct." Tielle gestures to the basket. "The child merely accepts what is, fantastic as it may seem. We should strive to be like him."

She doesn't say more, but her meaning is clear.

The divisions can't be missed. Arkonai, Bereft, and Saroth huddle in separate clumps scattered throughout the room.

Some tension melts away.

Lady Ireena crosses over to Tielle and strikes up a conversation.

"It's a start," says Marcus. "Marina would appreciate that fact."

Daniel can't muster any words, but he nods.

"You know I can understand your pain better than most." Marcus's words come out in low waves. He lays a hand on Daniel's shoulder. "That won't mean much to you right now, but when you're ready, I'm here for you."

The comfort conjures an image of Gabriella Polani, Marcus's wife, Katrina's mother, and Marina's adopted sister, who was murdered over a year ago. Daniel had tried to be a support for Marcus during that time, but now that he feels the full magnitude of losing his one true love, he understands the utter inadequacy of any gesture.

I finally understand you, Marcus, and I wish by the One I didn't.

They exchange a long, solemn look.

Marcus's hand slips off Daniel's shoulder.

"It's late," says Marcus. "Shall I start moving them out?"

"How is this done?" Daniel's question carries a rough edge. He tries to remember what happened with Gabriella, but his focus had been on consoling Marina. He recalls a funeral pyre surrounded by herbs and flowers. Every other detail eludes him. "The funeral. What do I do?"

Understanding brightens Marcus's eyes.

"You want the rites to be Saroth?" The question, though soft, has the power to drive the room into silence again.

"They will be both," Daniel replies, pouring as much strength into his voice as possible. "First Saroth, then Arkonai, but I don't have any idea how to arrange the first."

"Have you told Lady Corabelle?" Marcus asks urgently.

Daniel shakes his head, bewildered.

"You should," Tielle says. "I think she'd like to know."

"Don't worry about details. If you're sure about this, the Castaloni house will arrange everything for tomorrow evening," Marcus assures him.

"I will see to the arrangements myself, as soon as I have word from Lady Corabelle," says Mika Forester.

"Will she let me have the ashes?" Daniel feels exceedingly awkward asking the question.

"It's not tradition," Mika says softly, "but given the unique circumstances, I'd say there's a good chance she can be convinced."

"Speak with Gabriel if you need an ally in this," Tielle suggests. "He'll help."

Tielle and Raelyn circulate freely among the groups, offering fresh drinks, kind words, and hugs as necessary.

Daniel's grateful they're able to function through their grief. Someone brings him a wooden chair and eases him onto it. He spends untold minutes watching his daughter sleep, nestled beside Katrina's puppy form with young Tellen just outside the basket.

I wish you could see this, Marina.

"Lady Corabelle can see you now," says Mika.

Marcus smiles encouragement as Daniel slowly rises.

He tries to plan what to say, but when he reaches the bedroom threshold and sees Corabelle's stricken expression, words fail him.

"I will give you a moment," says Gabriel, slipping past Daniel.

Entering, Daniel shuts the door.

"Say what you must, Daniel." Lady Corabelle's intense green eyes stay fixed on Marina's still form. Silent tears fall, but she holds herself stiffly, visibly struggling to maintain her composure. "Have you decided ... where to bury her?"

The pain between them is palpable.

"Yes, but—" Daniel cuts himself off, knowing she won't hear him for a while anyway.

As Lady Corabelle's legs weaken, she moves to kneel, but Daniel catches her and pulls her into an embrace.

They cry together.

The hug is brief and awkward, but it breaks an unseen barrier between them. Daniel lowers Marina's mother onto a chair placed beside the bed and kneels so he can look up at her. A fading energy orb provides soft light. Holding Lady Corabelle's hands, Daniel speaks.

"Your daughter. My wife." Daniel swallows hard to gather the strength to continue. "Marina was the One's finest creation. She sought to heal everything from sickness to wounds to hatred. She was loved by many and should be honored by many. If you can arrange it, I believe she deserves Saroth and Arkonai funeral rites."

"You'd have only ashes to bury," Lady Corabelle points out. "That would never satisfy your people."

"It would satisfy me," Daniel insists. "My daughter is too young to care or understand, and Marina touched too many lives to cling to only one way. I will not deprive others of their chance to grieve, and she would be the first to protest her death causing division."

"I see why she chose you," Lady Corabelle comments, squeezing his hands before releasing them. She stands. "I will have Mika prepare the celebration of life ceremony. Come to the Castaloni estate here in Outreach tomorrow afternoon."

Chapter 1:
Lady Corabelle's Gift

Plains of Promise, Castaloni Estate near the City of Outreach
The night after Marina's death
(Vic is still eight months old)

A spectacular sunset creates a beautiful light show above. Daniel imagines that the fiery oranges and reds mixing with cooler blues and purples stand for the way Marina approached life: with passion and compassion.

Stepping from the garden paths to the Plains of Promise, he remembers the last two occasions that had brought him to this estate. Marcus and Gabriella's wedding reception had taken place in this exact spot many years ago, and a secondary funeral service for Gabriella had unfolded in a nearby field over a year ago. Marcus had known of Marina's inability to enter Caramore and insisted on a second ceremony for her sake.

Unconsciously, Daniel stops moving, closes his eyes, and taps into his Seeker Gifts. He usually can't read a field's history like he can a room, but his connection to the place and the people allows scenes from the wedding to play in his mind's eye. Gabriella's wedding dress had been nearly as wide around as she was tall, but she bounced from guest to guest hugging friends and strangers alike. Marina's expression that night had ranged from harried to distracted to overwhelmed because the party details fell to her to oversee, but she had occasionally found time to send him a sympathetic smile. As the only Arkonai present, the occasion hadn't been very comfortable for Daniel. His heart futilely longs to return to those moments, just to see Marina alive once more.

A small hand lands on Daniel's wet cheek, forcing his eyes to open. He stares down at familiar brilliant blue eyes. Vic offers him a toothy grin and babbles something nonsensical. Daniel holds her closer and kisses the top of her head. She squirms and twists her head about, fussing as she searches.

"She's not here." Daniel's throat tries to close around the words, as if keeping them in will lessen their impact.

Vic's whines ramp up into desperate wails. She flings her body left then right then back.

Daniel barely keeps her from launching out of his arms. Instinctively, he tightens his grip.

"Let me take her," says Raelyn, appearing beside Daniel. She holds out her arms to receive the baby.

Daniel hesitates, not sure he should subject another person to one of Vic's fits.

Vic kicks him in the gut and renews the assault on their ears.

Raelyn places a hand on the baby's back.

Vic turns her head to the side, shoves a thumb in her mouth, and leans against Daniel's shoulder.

"She'll be safe with me," Raelyn assures him. "Let yourself concentrate on the ceremony."

Reluctantly, Daniel pries Vic's hand off his shirt and turns her over to Raelyn. In a practiced move, the young woman settles the baby into a comfortable position. Daniel's arms feel light and empty without the baby, but he has enough wits to walk toward the crowd gathered a couple hundred paces across the field. Now that the sun has set completely, the torches lining the path at even intervals flare to life, showing Daniel the way.

Despite the numerous people present, Daniel has a clear path to the front. They've chosen a spot where the ground slopes downward, creating a natural amphitheater. More torches surround the entire area and mark out several sections. Energy orbs hover above the crowd, giving Daniel a clear view of the many colors present in the people's robes. Every step makes his heart beat harder and faster. Unlike Gabriella's celebration of life ceremony where his focus stayed with Marina, Daniel absorbs every detail and compares it to previous experiences with death.

His parents' funeral had been a small affair attended by several huntsmen who knew his father. The circumstances surrounding their deaths left the bodies unfit for being laid out in public. They had been buried as quickly as possible. Mourners wearing dark clothes or cloaks had filed past his father's greatsword and his mother's favorite shawl. Some knelt before the items and spoke quietly to them, but most paused a moment, bowed, and left a coin or two to pay for the burial.

The ceremony for Christa's parents differed mightily from that arranged for his parents due to the difference in their social status. Daniel cannot recall much of the many long speeches delivered that day, but he remembers sneaking up to the temple rafters with Jordan to peer down on their friend. So many people surrounded Christa Arrington the entire day, they couldn't approach her. The ceremony had stretched from dawn until midday and been unbearably hot.

Marcus, Tielle, and Gabriel had tried to explain what Daniel should expect tonight, but the sight of Marina's body lying on a comashure still shakes him. The Arkonai people have no equivalent word for the contraption. It's essentially a stone slab with a built-in depression for the body to rest upon. The closest thing Daniel can relate it to is a shallow bathtub.

Tielle had explained that sometimes a wall of evenly cut sticks will be arranged against the stone to mimic funeral pyres of the past, but it's more common to have flowers and herbs present. Somebody has arranged for the area surrounding the comashure to be lined with white lilies and red and white amaryllis flowers.

Daniel finds it fitting.

Tielle and Lady Corabelle have put Marina in a royal blue nightdress. A crown of tiny white flowers rests upon her head. Her hands lie folded across her stomach. He almost believes she's just sleeping.

Your position is to Lady Corabelle's left.

Daniel doesn't react to Marcus's instruction, but he sends silent thanks as he moves to the appropriate spot. A sidelong peek at Lady Corabelle reveals an expression of strained calm he understands perfectly. He glances away quickly but not before a burning sensation engulfs his eyes.

The murmur of side conversations cuts out completely.

Mika Forester moves behind Daniel and Lady Corabelle and greets the crowd.

Daniel hears the words but not one pierces the fog around his mind.

You may move forward and say a last farewell. I can

convey it to the witnesses or not as you desire.

You can share the words if you want.

Though warned he would get such an opportunity, every prepared word flees when the moment arrives. Nevertheless, Daniel steps forward and kneels on the cushion placed near Marina's head. The placement gives him a good view of her dark hair pooling around her head.

"Thank you for every moment of friendship and love. You changed more about me than I ever thought possible." Daniel pauses to swallow some sobs, forcing more words out past uncooperative lips. "I attacked you the first day we met, but you never held it against me." He smiles through the pain as he tries to memorize every one of her beautiful features. "You loved so many people so perfectly. I selfishly wish I had left this life first. You've done your part to protect Vic. I will not let that sacrifice be in vain, nor will I let her forget you. I will miss you every day, but be at peace, my love. We will meet again."

It takes much of Daniel's remaining willpower not to touch Marina, but that was the only consistent warning he received from everybody briefing him on the ceremony. Somehow, he stumbles back to his original position, and Lady Corabelle glides forward to kneel beside Marina.

Silence lingers and stretches.

Lady Corabelle has elected to share these final words only with her daughter.

Time passes.

The crowd maintains such a steady silence that Daniel hears night creatures moving through the plains and insects beating their wings nearby. Wind plays with the torchlight, changing the way the shadows move around Lady Corabelle and the comashure.

Help her up and offer her your hand, Daniel.

Marcus's instructions startle Daniel.

He barely has enough sense to obey. As if choreographed, Gabriel approaches from the other side. They reach Lady Corabelle simultaneously, grab an elbow, and raise her to a standing position.

Now, step back slowly.

The three of them retreat accordingly.

Release her and take a half-step left.

Daniel does so.

Gabriel moves right on the other side.

Daniel tries not to stare but fails.

You may focus on the lady as you like. The next move is hers.

Lady Corabelle bows her head and brings her hands down to her sides. Next, she curls her hands into fists, rotates her wrists outward, and snaps her fingers.

A small flame appears along the top of the comashure near Marina's head and spreads along the entire rim in a clockwise fashion.

The sound of a few hundred other snaps comes from behind Daniel.

By the time Lady Corabelle lifts her head, flames engulf Marina's body, creating an intense heat.

I apologize for the heat. We forgot to warn you about that. I know it's uncomfortable but try to stand still until it's over.

Sweat breaks out on Daniel's face, but he endures the increased heat. As the flames from the central fire burn hotter still, the torches lining the makeshift arena extinguish. His gaze flicks up to the torches. Faint smoke trails are visible in the moonlight.

This is the final phase. We call it the *New Dawn*. The fire is symbolically transformative, aiding the body's destruction so the soul will not linger. The phase can be as quick or slow as desired, but Lady Corabelle has elected for it to pass swiftly for Victoria's sake.

Vic.

The correction feels right to Daniel. He'd always preferred their daughter's full name. Always one to forge her own path, Marina had shortened it since day one. Now Daniel cannot imagine it any other way. It's a small thing, but he feels closer to Marina every time he thinks of Vic this way.

For Vic, for you, and because it fits the moment.

The intense heat makes breathing difficult. Daniel ponders Marcus's statement, but cannot grasp the full meaning. To distract himself, he tries to look into the fire but cannot.

It's almost over. Close your eyes. These are magic flames enhanced by almost every Saroth present. If you don't have that Gift, you could damage your sight by looking into such a fire.

Daniel bows his head and keeps his eyes closed until Marcus informs him the danger has passed. He expects to see the fire slowly diminish, but it vanishes in an instant, making Daniel flinch.

In life, Marina Castaloni-Saveron burned bright, but her light left this world too soon.

The torches return to normal brightness, and somebody releases several energy orbs over the central platform.

Daniel fixes his gaze on the comashure's edge, not daring to lift his eyes further for several heartbeats. When he finally works up the courage, he finds nothing. Painful alarm brings every sense alert.

It's all right! Just relax. Lady Corabelle has a gift for you. She is waiting for the crowd to disperse. They are moving to the reception back by the gardens. I'll meet you there later. You will be alone soon. Don't worry about Vic. Between Raelyn and Tielle, I doubt her feet will touch the ground tonight.

Fixing his attention on Marina's mother, Daniel waits patiently, noting the slight lift to her shoulders. The defensive, proud posture reminds him of Marina. Slowly, Lady Corabelle turns to Daniel. When she faces him fully, he's struck by how heavily Marina favored the lady in looks. The realization captivates him enough to make him miss the small, wooden box she clutches.

"This was her first creation," says Lady Corabelle. "She made it soon after discovering her Destroyer Gifts at age four. Her instructor said it was the most complicated task he offered. Most other children simply carved their name into a wooden slab and went to play. Not, Mari. She wanted a challenge." A hint of a smile forms as the lady holds the box out to Daniel. "She took almost two weeks to burn a hollow place into a block of wood to craft this. Master Parust said he tried to help her with the hinges, but she wouldn't let him."

Solemnly accepting the gift, Daniel examines the beautiful box.

"They're set just fine," he notes.

Lady Corabelle's smile flickers brighter.

"Antonio—her father—fixed them later on without telling her," she says, letting her hands fall to her sides. "I think Mari forgot about the box as soon as she gave it to me. That's how she was. Always off to take on a new adventure." Not satisfied with her current pose, Lady Corabelle lifts her hands and clasps them in front of her. "Where will you take her?"

"I built a cabin for us on the Karnok Mountains," Daniel replies.

As he prepares to elaborate, Lady Corabelle shakes her head.

"Say no more. I trust it is a peaceful place." The lady tips her chin up. "Take my daughter on one last adventure, huntsman. We will follow as soon as we can. There is much to discuss concerning Victoria's future."

Chapter 2:
A Hard Thing

Corabelle's Office, Castaloni Estate, City of Jorash
Two days after Marina's death
(Vic is still eight months old)

Corabelle doesn't hear the office door open, but the faint click as Mika Forester closes the door finally registers. She stands as formality demands, but when he waves for her to sit, she does so quickly, unsure of how long her legs would hold her anyway. Activating a privacy scroll, Corabelle tries to brace her nerves for the coming conversation. She's come to dread such meetings with the counselor and purser. In less than a decade, she has lost both her husband and her firstborn.

I envy you the peace of the next world, Antonio.

The many years since her husband's death has muted the pain, but this fresh wound is deeper and darker and even more difficult to bear because of its suddenness.

I wish you were here to help me bear this.

Corabelle immediately regrets the thought. Marina was her father's daughter through and through. Had he survived the lingering illness likely caused by poison, this would have utterly destroyed him.

"Have you read Marina's will?" Mika inquires, skipping formal greetings.

"I'm surprised she included Jackson, given the troubles between them," says Corabelle. "Did she ever confirm what caused the strife."

A glazed look passes over the counselor's face.

"You know I can't discuss that, even if I wanted to," says Mika, snapping out of his brief stupor. "Our dealings were conducted behind a privacy spell, same as this one." He motions to the spent scroll sitting on her desk.

"Your reaction has confirmed enough, and I do not require details." Sadness and weariness try to drain Corabelle's remaining strength. "It is enough to reinforce my decisions."

Mika sits up straighter.

"Do I need a recorder scroll?" he inquires.

"In a moment," Corabelle answers. "First, I'm going to give you the chance to talk me out of it."

"That would depend greatly upon what you've decided, my lady," Mika says, leaning forward eagerly. "As with Antonio's will, I have filed Marina's changes, but they are within my grasp to alter, amend, or retract as necessary. What would you like me to do?"

"Amend." Corabelle lets the word stand alone for a short time before elaborating. "I have not spoken with Daniel yet, but given his nature, I can predict his response. Victoria cannot inherit the holdings until she comes of age, and I think it best her formal education in such matters be postponed until that time."

"That would leave the companies vulnerable for upwards of two decades," Mika points out.

"Not if she has a sponsor or a manager to act on her behalf," says Corabelle.

"As is, that means Daniel Saveron, Marcus Polani, Jackson, Gabriel, and finally, you."

"Add in a clause that stipulates a married couple be given higher consideration when the vote for Victoria's sponsor goes before the house council."

Confusion clouds Mika's face, but it soon clears.

"You intend for Gabriel to run the holdings," says Mika.

"For all intents and purposes, he's done such since Antonio's death," Corabelle explains. "It's time he reaps some of the benefits for that work."

"Jackson will sue for control again," Mika warns.

Corabelle waves the concern away.

"His last attempt was half-hearted at best," she says. "I think he's in love with the idea of control. He cares nothing for the businesses. I doubt he even knows how many companies belong to the holdings or what they do."

"Do you not fear his ambition?"

"Jackson's an academic, not a business-minded man," says Corabelle, ignoring the true meaning of the counselor's question. She'll ponder it in private later. "Gabriel's more like their father. He'll keep the businesses on a solid path."

"What of Daniel Saveron and Marcus Polani?" asks Mika. "Like Jackson, they hold a position ahead of Gabriel in the succession."

"That is the second amendment we must add," says Corabelle. "The role of guardian and sponsor must be allowed to split if necessary. Marina alluded to this, but I want it clarified. Daniel is a huntsman. I cannot see him quitting the Guild to run Saroth businesses, nor can I imagine he'd suffer anybody raising his daughter. As for Marcus, so long as Victoria is safe, I doubt he'd quit his work for the Academy of Arts and Sciences."

"This will put Gabriel and Tielle in danger." Mika levels a hard look at Corabelle. "In multiple ways. Are you willing to do that?"

"What choice do I have?" Corabelle meets his intense gaze. "I cannot in good conscience subject the holdings to Jackson's rule when I know Gabriel can keep them flourishing. At this point, he's had many years dealing with standard house intrigue."

"I'm not talking about that," Mika says. "If I know you, you've had the River's Edge affair investigated."

"I didn't need to," Corabelle confesses, feeling an old chill creep over her soul. "Gabriel explained enough. He's many things, but a keeper of secrets is not one of them."

Mika's expression is difficult to read, but he finally dispenses with subtleties.

"Do you not fear Jackson will see Gabriel and his intended as threats and move against them?"

"I want to believe he's changed." Corabelle strives to drive doubts from her voice, but the declaration comes out soft and wistful. "But that brings us to the third amendment."

"Marina put in safeguards for the holdings in the event Jackson gains control of them," says Mika, looking resigned. "If he changes something significant, the holdings can go public. While Victoria remains heir, he'd be barred from making any drastic decisions anyway. That will cripple the growth. Gabriel's provisions have no such limitations. That's going to anger Jackson. What more can we do to make him leave well enough alone?"

"Change the percentages and terms," says Corabelle.

"Marina's shares automatically go in trust for her daughter. Seal off the funds except for a monthly allotment for Daniel to care for her. He likely won't accept it. After a year, make those funds available to the sponsor only if he or she can produce Victoria at the time of the withdrawal. If something happens to Victoria, give the managers the option to depart. If something happens to her primary sponsor, responsibility falls to the secondary sponsor. If both cannot fulfill their duties, a new primary will be elected, but this time, the position comes with only a small stipend in addition to normal managerial rates."

"That's a bold move, my lady," Mika comments.

"It encourages all parties to see that Gabriel, Tielle, and Victoria survive the next two decades," says Corabelle. "That is the best protection I can give them."

"And what of your own protection?" Mika inquires.

"I've recently acquired an alternate voting position for the Tariku League, so I will spend most of my time in Dominance."

"Congratulations."

"Thank you," says Corabelle. "I'm on mandatory leave for a month to mourn properly, and I have permission to stretch that to a year if necessary. I'm hoping the work will allow me to move on." She attempts a smile with only marginal results. "I'm ready to move on without messy house business."

Mika agrees to the amendments and clarification statements for Marina's will.

They spend the next half-hour working through various wordings before making the record official.

As soon as Mika departs to file the amended will with the Tariku League, Corabelle has a servant summon Gabriel and Tielle.

Soon, the couple enters, looking more than a little haggard.

Gabriel's eyes dart around the room, a nervous habit he picked up from his squirrel form.

Abandoning her desk, Corabelle embraces her youngest child. He stands stiffly, but she can feel the charged magic currents swirling around him. He's barely refraining from cycling his Shapeshifter forms.

When the embrace ends, Corabelle holds out a hand toward Tielle Toscano. The young woman accepts the hand and starts to curtsey, but Corabelle pulls her upright.

"Please. We are far beyond that," says Corabelle. "You are my son's intended and the closest I've ever come to having an apprentice.

Be seated, and I will explain myself."

Force of habit makes Tielle dip her head, but she allows Corabelle to lead her over to a pair of comfortable chairs.

Gabriel reluctantly sits down, but he stays perched on the edge, right leg bouncing. Tielle grips his left hand and squeezes, quelling the nervous gesture.

The interaction encourages Corabelle. She explains the situation as swiftly and thoroughly as possible.

Gabriel blinks at her.

"You want us to move the wedding up?" He glances uncertainly at Tielle.

"To this afternoon if possible," Corabelle replies.

"We can't," Gabriel protests. His voice has more strength this time. "The mourning period for Marina has barely begun."

"We cannot celebrate properly at this time," Corabelle admits, "but nothing stands against conducting the legal ceremony, especially given the will's provisions. Daniel must find something to save Victoria, and we must give him the time to do so. The Tariku League will not let her stay in Caramore without house sponsors. The only question is your willingness to accept such responsibilities."

"Jack's not going to like it," Gabriel mutters.

That is an understatement.

"Leave him to me," says Corabelle. "The house council can meet as early as tomorrow. If you wed today and petition to become Victoria's sponsors tomorrow, you should get the position as soon as Daniel and Marcus lay down their rights."

Both Tielle and Gabriel look stunned.

"Do you want this?" Gabriel asks Tielle.

The young woman's eyes flit between Gabriel and Corabelle.

"This is very sudden," she comments.

Corabelle kneels before the couple, gazing at each intently.

"I am without a doubt placing you in grave danger, but you are Victoria's best chance of living long enough to claim her inheritance." Corabelle pauses to let the statement sink past their collective shock. "This is the second significant death we've suffered in a decade. We must quickly prove our house is strong, or those wishing to climb past us will go through us."

"They would go after Vic?" Tielle sounds horrified. "She's a baby."

Corabelle nods but forges on, not wishing to dwell on the

prospect of unknown enemies attacking her granddaughter. An alternative occurs to her, bringing a mixture of sorrow and longing.

"I have asked a hard thing of you, but you have other options," says Corabelle, standing to relieve a burning sensation in her legs.

Gabriel's gaze sharpens. He goes completely still as another animal instinct kicks in.

"You can leave the holdings to your brother's limited control or sell them off and store the proceeds for Victoria," Corabelle explains. "Either option would be easier and safer for everybody. We have enough combined wealth to sustain us for several years, and the sale proceeds would make that many years, more if you keep expenses low."

"No," says Tielle.

"No?" Gabriel questions.

"We are not leaving your sister's child defenseless before house politics," Tielle declares, glaring at Gabriel. She faces Corabelle. "We will do what's necessary, Lady Corabelle. Vic will have a sponsor."

"Her father's a huntsman. She's not exactly defenseless," says Gabriel, peering fondly at his intended. "But we are of one mind on this. We will sponsor Vic before the house council."

Corabelle turns away to finalize some details for the hasty wedding. As Gabriel and Tielle exit to find more suitable clothes, Corabelle watches them go. Part of her wishes to stop them and give Tielle one more chance to walk away, but she cannot bring herself to do so. Ages ago, her husband's aunt had warned her of the dangers involved in marrying so far above her station. She'd ignored the advice.

Do I regret it? Would I choose differently if I knew what the future would hold for us?

It doesn't take Corabelle long to reject the idea. Even the crushing weight of losing Marina cannot completely obliterate the joy of watching her grow up.

I will try to protect your daughter, Mari, but as usual, you've made things difficult.

In spite of new pain, the thought makes Corabelle smile.

Chapter 3:
Revelations and Experiments

Jackson's Study, Fort Medron
Three days after Marina's death
(Vic is still eight months old)
Marina's dead.

None of the hundreds of ways Jackson Castaloni imagined bringing about that event came close to what transpired. Up to that point, the plan had unfolded as designed. He'd had Barsi fetch Marina's apprentice, Raelyn Cordova, and traded the young woman's life for his sister's cooperation.

Bitter laughter pops out of Jackson.

You always chose your own path. You didn't have to die. We would have let the Healer live. Why would you sacrifice your strength for anybody, let alone an Arkonai?

I told you. She did it for her daughter. She believed I would kill the baby at the first opportunity.

"Will you?" Jackson wonders, glancing around. He's spent the last hour lost in thought, ignoring his studies. "Kill the child?"

Of course, but as before, events must transpire in a certain order. I must be able to leave this prison and stand on Aeris with full access to my powers if we hope to subdue the land properly. For that, I require the magic bracers. We are close to them. I can feel it.

"Daniel won't begin the search for a couple of days," says Jackson. "He's burying Marina's ashes somewhere in the Karnok Mountains. After that, he'll have to play the loyal huntsman and obtain leave from Guild duties before he can take up the quest for the bracers." Jackson lets his frustration ring through his next statement. "He may not even begin at that point, unless my mother prevails upon him to leave Victoria with my brother."

Why does that irritate you?

"Gabriel's younger," Jackson explains. "That was my problem with Marina. Why should he be able to skip ahead of me simply because he's married?" His irritation becomes anger, manifesting in a small fireball, which he hurls toward the fireplace. It splashes against the brick frame and dissipates.

I thought you had laid down the desire to control the Castaloni holdings. You gain almost as much wealth from them as if you had full control without any of the work required in maintaining their viability. I view that as a bargain.

"It's the principle of the matter," Jackson mutters. "Besides, if I do ever inherit, it will be in name only. Marina and Mika saw to that."

If you truly desire this, kill your brother and his new wife.

"I can't. They're my only means to an heir." Jackson's surprised that the idea doesn't bother him anymore. Many years ago, his master had informed him that powerful magic comes at a price. In other words, his studies into forbidden magic have cost him the ability to produce an heir naturally.

All things in due course, my young servant. I reward those who are loyal to me. First, we must obtain the bracers. Then, we can kill Victoria. After that, we can raise an unstoppable army of undead, cultivate Arkonai and Saroth servants to stir up a war, wait for the chaos to remove our enemies, and at last, rule this world as it was meant to be ruled.

Jackson's heart falters when confronted with the enormity of the tasks. He doesn't like relying on others, but he lacks the Gifts to accomplish everything alone.

Do not be dismayed at the work that lies ahead. Think of what you have accomplished. You have brought down a Supreme Huntmaster and indirectly cultivated another. Jordan Lekros may be of further use to us in the future. I will keep you apprised of my thoughts if I find a use for him.

Instead of picturing the current Supreme Huntmaster of the Arkonai Hunting Guild, Jackson's thoughts wander to the man's wife. His time in Lady Christa Arrington's presence had been brief, but at any moment, he can clearly recall everything about her from shimmering golden hair to blue gown to expression of deep-seated sadness. This was mere moments before she pledged herself to Jordan Lekros to gain justice for her uncle's murder.

I see your desire for the Arkonai woman has not diminished over the years, but put such thoughts out of your head. As with her husband, I have not yet formulated how she may be of use to me, but her many connections are worth considering.

A fluttering, restless feeling comes over Jackson, evidence of his master's distraction.

"What connections?" Jackson inquires.

Her daughter for one, and her connection to Daniel Saveron for another.

"I thought the Supreme Huntmaster had a son," says Jackson, though he'd be the first to admit not really keeping up with Arkonai births and deaths.

He does, but he does not know Lady Christa had twins.

"Why would she hide something like that?"

Her motives do not matter. What matters is the girl. Dina. She's only a child, not even seven years old, but there's power in her. Moreover, there's an opportunity to sow seeds of resentment for her lot in life.

"She's part of the most powerful Arkonai family," Jackson points out. He conjures a small flame and changes its shape so it can weave between his fingers. "What has she to resent, especially at such a young age?"

A tingling sensation crawls across his chest, conveying his master's amusement even as a deep chuckle echoes in his mind.

You are thinking as a Saroth, but Arkonai do not think as your people do. That is why I have chosen you. The girl's entire existence is a secret. Her mother barely tolerates her seeing the light of day. She has no real friends, only tutors and servants. It isn't much, but it may be enough to make her our ally.

"Why do we need such allies?" Jackson wonders. "Will not an undead army be enough?"

Armies must move about freely to be effective, but do not worry about such details yet. The prisoners have awakened. Give them sustenance and prepare for the summoning ritual. Today, we will learn if Bereft lives are as useful as those touched by magic.

Jackson had forgotten about the prisoners obtained on the road between the village of Kesh and the city of Castleton. Normally, he hunts in the poor sections of Arkonai cities or purchases prisoners from a neutral city. He's even ambushed those foolish enough to wander the Badlands or the Ashlands. He had always assumed the boost he obtained by siphoning another's life energy required them to be blessed with some magical Gift. He's never been so intrigued by the prospect of being wrong. A shortage of able-bodied supports has hampered him for years, but if Bereft lives will suffice, he can move his studies forward by leaps and bounds.

Letting the flame disappear, he conjures himself into the combat arena, aiming for the center. The sand shifts beneath his feet as he appears.

The man and woman stare at him. Jackson doesn't need to see the terror on their faces. The entire arena reeks of their fear and pain. The Transportation scroll had not been kind to them, resulting in the man fracturing both legs and the woman breaking an arm upon delivery. Since they had passed out from the journey, Jackson had arranged the chains so they could reach the ground. He'd even been kind enough to only bind the woman's unbroken arm. He hadn't bothered chaining the child since he couldn't find a suitable manacle. Instead, he had tethered the boy's waist with a leather cord attached to a hook on the wall.

Somehow, the child had slipped free from the restraint.

The entire family huddles together with the couple seated side-by-side and the child clinging fiercely to the woman.

Stop staring. Heal their wounds and feed them.

Knowing his mother always has the cook in their Jorash estate maintain a table for him, Jackson summons a loaf of fresh bread, a pot of vegetable stew, three cups of water, and appropriate bowls and utensils, directing them to appear on a tray beside the Bereft man.

The prisoner eyes the offering warily but makes no move to take it.

"Eat," Jackson orders. "I need you to be healthy for my ritual to work."

"We'll not help ya," declares the man.

This is tedious. Threaten the child.

Jackson conjures a dagger and holds it up for his prisoners to see.

"You will help me because the other option is that I end your son's life with this blade."

"Spare him," pleads the woman. "Please, he canna harm ya. He's just a wee lad."

22

Confirm the bargain. Put the dagger away and call forth the Healing scrolls.

Following the instructions, Jackson tucks the dagger into a sheath hidden in his robes and pulls three Healing scrolls from the Veil. It's wasteful, but he can afford it.

"If you obey, I will leave him in an orphanage when this is over," Jackson promises.

"So, ye do intend ta kill us, ya devil," says the man.

"The ritual requires sacrifice," Jackson replies. It's a lie, but he hasn't the time to explain the nuances of needing their lifeforces to sustain his magical abilities long enough to complete the complicated portal creation spell.

"We'll do it." The woman weaves conviction into her tone.

"No, Ellie," argues the man. "'Tis better he shares our fate."

The woman whirls on her husband, causing the chains to rattle. The movement jostles her injured arm, but the pain in her expression disappears in favor of fury.

"We'll not be sacrificin' our son's life fer pride, Aiden McDowell. If there's a chance ta spare him, we'll be takin' it an' that's that. Mark me words."

"Aye, so be it," agrees the man. His features harden as he turns his eyes from the woman back to Jackson. "Swear ta spare the lad by the One and the Lady."

Do it.

In reflection of his master's feelings, a wave of disgust twists Jackson's stomach about uncomfortably. Nevertheless, he chokes out the oath.

In keeping with their end of the bargain, the couple dutifully applies the Healing scrolls. Next, they eat the food Jackson summons for them while he reviews the phrases involved in the ritual. He even conjures a selection of pastries to share when they finish the bread and stew. His stomach complains about neglect, especially with the tempting scent of stew filling the arena, but he needs his personal energy levels to be low in order to discover if the Bereft lifeforces can sustain him.

Once the feeding and healing tasks are complete, Jackson moves the woman to a position directly across from the man and chains them both to the wall. The boy clings to the woman's left leg.

Before Jackson can utter a word, the woman pleads with him.

"Have mercy. Please."

"I've already agreed to spare the boy." Jackson gives the lady a questioning look.

She does not want him to witness the ritual. It's probably a good idea. One never truly knows what can imprint on a child. Do you have a sleep scroll? You'll also need a personal nullifier to avoid drawing from the boy.

Though not pleased by yet another delay, Jackson fetches the appropriate scrolls from his office. He might have pulled a sleep scroll from the Veil, but it's better to grab the one he'd neglected to use last night. He needs to search his office safe for the Null scroll anyway. This experiment is becoming very costly.

The knowledge will be worth it.

After applying the scrolls to the Bereft boy, Jackson finally starts the ritual. In theory, the complicated spell should allow his master's spirit to come out of the Veil and stay anchored on Aeris.

The ritual fails its primary objective but answers the secondary question concerning Bereft lifeforces. By the end, the woman has perished, and the man has only the faintest spark of life within him.

Jackson moves to finish the man, but trips and lands hard on his hands and knees.

Rest from your labors. When you recover, we can discuss the findings.

The fact that Jackson completed the ritual proves he can work under such conditions. Conversely, the pain raging in his head, coupled with a trembling throughout his body, illustrates the point that the energy received is not as effective.

The child.

Jackson's arms collapse. He barely has enough sense to turn his head left to avoid landing on his nose. He falls on his side facing the child.

You can deal with that issue later as well. Sleep.

An irresistible urge to sleep wraps warmly around Jackson's mind.

Chapter 4:
Layer of Protection

Marina's Final Resting Place, Karnok Mountains near Daniel's Cabin
Three days after Marina's death
(Vic is still eight months old)

I'd meant to do this alone, but as you can see, too many people loved you for me to get away with that. I'll come back later. I promise.

Kneeling before his wife's grave, Daniel picks up a handful of dirt and places it atop the small wooden box holding Marina's ashes. Resisting the urge to touch the box one last time, he stands and moves a few paces away so others can offer a few last words and help with the burial by adding more dirt. He's close enough to hear those who wish to speak aloud, but far enough to give those who wish it the necessary privacy.

The crowd comes nowhere near the number of people present at the Saroth celebration of life ceremony two nights ago, but Daniel's touched that even this many made the long journey up the Karnok Mountains.

In accordance with Arkonai customs, those not currently before the grave form a line that weaves through the forest. Though Marcus Polani could not make the journey with his young daughter, he sent Navina Christol to oversee the details of keeping guests informed of the protocol. Daniel hasn't seen the Minder in several years, not since the search for the Arkonai Hunting Guild's stolen treasury funds came to a violent conclusion. She stands on the opposite side ready to direct mourners as needed.

The first couple to approach after Daniel is Emeric and Olivia Cordova, Raelyn's parents. They stoop to add dirt but do not linger. The same holds true for Raelyn's brother, Ethan, and his family. Raelyn spends more time kneeling before the grave, but Daniel wouldn't be surprised if she joins him later after the crowds have gone. She doesn't speak until she regains her feet.

"Thank you for everything. It was an honor to learn from you. Though I was the one blessed with the Healing Gift, you showed me how to use it best." Raelyn's tears drip down onto the dirt in the shallow pit. Sniffling, she draws several shuddering breaths. "I don't know what you did or how you did it, but I know I stand here today because of you. I said it several nights ago, and I'll say it again. I will help Daniel save Vic. You have my word."

When Raelyn finally scrambles to her feet and trots over to speak with her parents, four young men take her place. They form a tight semi-circle around the grave. Daniel can only see two of their faces because two have their backs to him, but their clothes catch his eye. Two wear plain, earth-toned Arkonai attire, and two wear flowing Saroth robes.

"You probably wouldn't remember me, Lady Marina," says one of the young Arkonai men. "My name is Erlo. A few years ago, you saved my life and sent Lady Raelyn to Heal my mum. I never got to thank you properly, and I'm sorry for that. Finley made me come. We also brought Gio and Jace. We're all mates now, and I suspect that's your doing too. Gonna let the others have their say now."

"Finley here," says the other Arkonai man. Unlike his companion, he kneels and adds his handful of dirt before continuing his speech. "Don't have much to say, but I hope you're in a better place. The world could use more people like you."

The Saroth eye each other, silently working out who will go first. Finally, the one standing directly across from Daniel elbows his friend to take his turn.

The chosen one rubs his ribs and frowns before sitting beside the hole.

"I never told you my full name. It's Giovanel Lastra. My father had a disagreement with his older brother, so we left Caramore to live in Temperance. Been Gio a long time. Let's just say I wasn't at my best when we met, but your kindness to all of us helped. I don't always agree with Arkonai, but Finley had a point. May the One guide you to a better place, Lady Marina."

The last Saroth man sits by the grave for almost a minute, silently delivering his sentiments.

Next, Callen and Ireena bring Tellen forward. The boy looks at them uncertainly, watching carefully as they scoop up some loose dirt and place it on the box. Eager to follow their lead, he picks up two handfuls of dirt. Anticipating this, Callen and Ireena each catch an arm and guide it into place to complete the delivery.

Kyle Ricci and his new wife, Syanna, step forward as Callen and Ireena escort Tellen away from the intriguing mound of dirt. After kneeling together, the dark-skinned couple bows their heads and clasp hands. Their attire interests Daniel because it's simple enough to be Bereft, but he can feel magic flowing through them. They are quiet so long that Daniel expects them to spend their time allotment in silence, but eventually, Kyle speaks.

"I'll miss you, Sparks. You had more love for people than anybody I've ever known and less social sense as well. You were a brilliant Destroyer as a kid and an even better healer later. You'll be happy to know I'm still applying the Gift to diseases as you taught me all those years ago. Be safe in the next life."

Annie Kerns spends her time weeping, and afterwards, she places a small scroll into the grave.

One last letter from Christa.

Navina takes her turn. Daniel expects her time to be brief since she didn't really know Marina, but it stretches longer than most. He wonders why until he remembers she is there on Marcus's behalf, and they're both Minders.

I apologize for the delay. I've asked Navina to recite a passage from one of the holy books, but she's never seen it before. I've only seen it once, and I didn't bother committing it to memory. Navina has a friend searching the Alamon Temple archives for it.

What passage?

The part I wanted her to read concerns the One's original design for Aeris and how far we've fallen from that ideal.

I'm sure she would appreciate that. Thank you.

I'm sorry I couldn't make it. Katrina and I will journey there in the future once you settle things with Victoria.

The talk with Marcus prevents Daniel from hearing the beginning of what Tielle and Gabriel say, but he tunes in as they sit Vic in the grass beside the hole. The baby leans forward, hands outstretched to reach the box, but Tielle scoops her up and wraps her in a tight embrace before reaching for Gabriel's hand.

"Mika sends his regrets for not coming. He's handling the rest of the house council and the managers this week. Mother's not far away in the cabin Daniel built for you, which is beautiful by the way. You would like it, and it's probably more spacious than your home in Outreach. I think Mother will be by later, but she's not ready to face another crowd of strangers. You know how she is." Gabriel taps the fingers of his right hand on his leg. His other hand is still firmly attached to his wife's hand. "Tielle and I got married the day after your celebration of life ceremony. It wasn't anything like you would have planned, but it still counts. We can be Vic's sponsors before the house council. I … wish it wasn't necessary, but you know I'd do anything for you. You were, and always will be, my hero as well as my sister. I love you and can't wait to see you again. Before I go, I want to show you a trick."

With that, Gabriel stands and flips through his various Shapeshifter forms. He becomes a beetle and lands on the mound of dirt covering the box. Then, he flies to the edge and becomes a squirrel. Dashing up the nearest tree, he emerges triumphantly with an acorn. He leaves the top piece as a gift beside Tielle who places it onto the box. Finally, Gabriel takes on his wolf form and lays down beside the grave, whining low. Upon returning to human form, he brushes the remaining dirt into the hole and pats it down.

The rest of the morning and most of the afternoon pass quickly as guests mingle in and out of Daniel's cabin. Lady Corabelle and several Castaloni servants arranged for plenty of food and drinks. A few people left early, but most who stayed slip away at some point to spend more time making peace with their pain at Marina's final resting place. As the host, Daniel cannot leave, so he will have his moment alone after the guests depart.

When only Raelyn, Lady Corabelle, Tielle, Gabriel, and Vic remain, Daniel herds them to the common room and gathers their attention. He notices Gabriel and Tielle have exchanged their dirty robes for clean ones. He didn't think they'd brought any clothes. The point confuses him until his eyes fall upon Lady Corabelle, and he remembers that both she and Tielle are Conjurers. Marina's mother looks weary beyond words. She has been using her Gifts frequently throughout the day.

"What is on your mind, Daniel?" asks Lady Corabelle.

"I want to put an open-ended contract on my daughter," says Daniel.

Everybody—including Vic—stares blankly at him. She sits on Tielle's lap, sucking her thumb.

"How would that work?" asks Gabriel.

"I guess I need to explain myself," Daniel says with a wry smile.

"It would help," says Raelyn. "I don't think any of us knows much about Seeker Gifts."

"What do you need from us?" inquires Tielle.

Daniel doesn't understand everything it means that Gabriel and Tielle can now sponsor Vic, but he gathers there's some legal power behind the appointment.

"The type of contract I wish to make with Vic requires consent, but as family, you can answer for her in these matters," Daniel explains. Opening the Veil, he removes the contract he'd prepared and tosses it to Gabriel.

The younger man flinches upon catching it, likely surprised by the enchanted contract. He passes the scroll to Tielle who gives it to Raelyn to deliver to Lady Corabelle. Vic watches the proceedings with interest.

"Many Seekers and Guardians possess the ability to write protection contracts like that one," says Daniel. "Teleporting is not a primary part of our Gifts, but many have it as a secondary skill. Normally, we're only allowed one open contract at a time, but this type is an exception because it only activates in moments of extreme peril for the one being protected."

"Did you have such a contract with Marina?" asks Lady Corabelle.

Her sharp look warns Daniel against answering, but he nods anyway.

She covers her mouth and flees the cabin, leaving stunned silence in her wake.

Vic cries.

What's wrong? What'd I say?

The contract you described casts new light on your account of Marina's death.

Marcus's thought sounds supportive, but it has an edge that makes Daniel wary.

When the full implication hits, Daniel staggers.

It's my fault. The Dark Man wanted me there. He wasn't just there by accident. He stabbed her because of the contract.

It's not your fault.

This time, Marcus's thought lacks conviction.

"Set up the contract," says Raelyn.

"Will it place her in more danger?" Tielle adjusts her grip on Vic.

"It will allow Daniel to answer danger that arises," Raelyn replies, facing Tielle. She whirls on Daniel. "And Marina's death was not your fault."

"Would she have been there, if not for me?" Daniel wonders, fearing the answer.

"It doesn't matter," says Lady Corabelle from the cabin's threshold. "Victoria will be pursued by many people for many reasons, including her connection to the Castaloni name." She addresses these words to all, but her last ones target Daniel. "If you can add a layer of protection, do so."

She holds out the crinkled contract.

Before his courage can fail, Daniel withdraws an ink and quill set from the Veil and presents the contract to Gabriel and Tielle for signing. He follows this by obtaining signatures from Raelyn and Lady Corabelle as witnesses. Before he can search the Veil for funds to pay for the contract, Lady Corabelle conjures a gold coin. He considers protesting but reason prevails. Taking the coin, Daniel retrieves the contract from Raelyn and presses the money to the scroll.

"With this contract, I pledge to protect Victoria Amaryllis Saveron with all my strength and skill until my life ends or this contract is no longer needed. I will be her Guardian when no other can be found. May the Lady's light and grace guide our every step."

The coin and scroll disappear into the Veil to be filed with the Arkonai Hunting Guild's recordkeeper later.

"You hear that, Vic?" Tielle asks the baby. "Your daddy will always protect you."

He'll try very hard anyway.

You will.

Vic yawns, stretches, and mumbles something before stuffing a fist into her mouth and closing her eyes.

"She's very taken with the idea," Gabriel reports. Grinning, he places an arm around Tielle's shoulders.

With the contract settled, Daniel's attention turns to the next task: finding the fabled bracers that can keep Vic from turning into one of the undead. Marina's last gift and other magical interventions can only last so long.

Chapter 5:
You Knew

Castaloni Estate, City of Jorash
Four days after Marina's death
(Vic is still eight months old)

"Go to sleep," Gabriel orders.

Tielle Castaloni smiles at the change in her husband's voice. It's always deeper in wolf form.

"I've tried. I can't. I've been staring at the ceiling forever," says Tielle, sitting up on the bed. "Maybe I should check on Vic again."

"She's fine," Gabriel insists. "Your last check was hardly ten minutes ago."

"Come sit with me." Tielle swings her legs over the side, leaving room next to her. The motion causes the dim energy orbs to brighten, making her squint. She pats the bed invitingly. "You can stay in the grumpy wolf form if it makes you feel better."

Gabriel regards her suspiciously before trotting over and sitting in front of her.

"I don't think you understand the nature of this guarding business." He stops speaking when she scratches the top of his head. Taking his human form, Gabriel catches her hand and gives her a pleading look. "Tielle—"

"Don't say it," Tielle snaps, snatching her hand away. Her frustration spikes, bringing hot tears to the surface. She glares at her husband.

"I need—"

"What you need is to let people in, Gabriel Castaloni." Tielle tries to stem the tide of words, but they flow out of her in a rush along with the tears. "I'm your best friend. More than that, I'm your wife, and you're shutting me out because you're shutting everybody out. I know this is the worst week you've faced since your father's death. I didn't know your sister half as well as you did, and I feel like I've been run through with a sword. Talk to me! What are you thinking? What are you feeling? What do you need from me?"

Sitting beside her, Gabriel wraps her in a comforting hug, compounding her sense of guilt.

"I'm sorry," says Tielle. "I shouldn't be adding to your burden. I'm just tired of feeling useless."

Chuckling, Gabriel tightens his grip and kisses the top of her head.

"I don't deserve you." His voice has a reflective quality. "That's what I'm thinking." Pulling away, he tips her chin up and kisses her lips. "I love you. That's what I'm feeling." Regret crosses his handsome face. His green eyes shift to a smoky gray color.

Alarm charges through Tielle. She's only seen his eyes shift color a few other times. The last shift to this color was when his mother told him of his father's death.

"But it's not all that you're feeling," Tielle says, suddenly insecure. "There's also regret and fear." She's too terrified of his answer to continue.

Do you regret marrying me?

"Do you regret marrying me?" Gabriel's voice matches the vulnerable expression on his face. His eyes shift back to their normal shade of green.

Tielle smiles as he echoes her question. Cupping his face, she plants a lingering kiss on his lips.

"Marrying you will never be one of my regrets," she promises. "Why would you say such a thing?"

"My family's a mess," says Gabriel. "My brother's a recluse. My sister's been murdered, likely by a dark spirit who wants something from her husband. My mother somehow thinks I can protect my niece from unseen evils. Did I miss anything? I can't help thinking I'm going to get you killed."

Mention of Vic makes Tielle glance over at the crib set along the wall opposite the bed. Gabriel's childhood room has hardly changed since the days he used it. The spacious room could probably fit her former bedroom three times over. Two sets of wide windows have built-in shelves overflowing with toys and stuffed animals, freshly conjured there by Lady Corabelle for Vic's entertainment. Once Gabriel became a teenager, he spent more days and nights at their Outreach or Dominance estates learning everything he could about the businesses. Though Tielle's position doesn't allow her to see the baby's face, she can clearly recall every feature.

"How could anybody even consider harming her?" Tielle wonders, ignoring Gabriel's confession. She honestly doesn't know how to answer him.

"People do a lot for money or power," Gabriel points out. "Jack was willing to attack Marina once upon a time to gain the inheritance."

I don't think I'll ever trust your brother, and you probably shouldn't either, dear heart.

Not wishing to spark an argument, Tielle dodges the mention of Gabriel's brother. Her husband's good nature and capacity to forgive far outstrips her own. In unguarded moments, she can still feel the enchanted ropes Jackson Castaloni bound her with to prove a point years ago. He'd also forced her to wear a necklace enchanted with a tracking charm for nearly six months. As a result, she avoids necklaces except for very special occasions. Jackson had shown up at Marina's celebration of life ceremony, but thankfully not spoken to them.

"We may not have much influence over the Tariku League, but the laws are such that Vic's life is closely linked to the holdings," Gabriel continues, heedless of her distraction. "Some people see that as a great opportunity to earn a quick payout."

"Would the holdings pay a ransom?" Tielle inquires. "I thought Marina changed those provisions?"

"She did," says Gabriel, "but my mother would pay. I would pay. There are always ways around such provisions, which is why it's still a valid concern."

Why didn't Lady Corabelle visit Vic more often when Marina was alive?

Grateful her husband is a Shapeshifter and not a Minder, Tielle buries that thought too. Technically, marriage to Gabriel gives her the right to address Lady Corabelle familiarly, but Tielle still has much of the servant mentality ingrained in her. Unofficially training in the Conjuring arts with Lady Corabelle has helped her overcome some social boundaries, but some things will never change. She also has no wish to stir up trouble.

Before Tielle can comment, a sharp shift in the room's magic currents brings her up off the bed.

Gabriel shifts into wolf form and bounds over to the crib. Spinning around, he growls low.

Three men wearing dark robes appear. The center man holds a Teleportation scroll, which he drops to the ground. The other two men grasp the first man's shoulders, allowing them to travel with the one in control of the Teleportation scroll.

What happened to the wards?

Teleporting directly into an estate should only be possible within certain rooms, but Tielle doesn't get to ponder the mystery.

The low-level energy orbs wink out, casting the room into darkness.

A bright light flashes.

A lightning bolt strikes Tielle squarely in the chest, flinging her into the wall above the bed. The personal shield she'd donned earlier upon Lady Corabelle's insistence collapses completely, having done its job. Tielle crashes hard onto the bed and rolls off as a second lightning bolt sets the bed on fire. Using the Saroth Gift for fire, Tielle smothers the flames before they can spread. Dizzy from the effort, she staggers to her feet.

A new energy orb provides enough light to see Gabriel valiantly fighting the three men. One assailant lies on the ground, howling as blood flows from his left leg. The second man struggles to hold Gabriel's thrashing wolf form, and the third tries to edge around them to get to Vic's crib.

Desperate, Tielle drops down to her knees and uses her Gift to summon every doll she saw in the storage room. After directing the dolls into the crib, Tielle conjures a thick mist and has it engulf the entire crib.

Vic wakes up and cries, but Tielle steels her heart and thickens the cloud filling the room.

A sharp yelp nearly freezes Tielle's heart. Fear prevents her from speaking, but terrifying sounds reach her.

Men grunt, curse, and cry out in pain.

A thud sounds, and there's less noise.

Another thud sounds, and there's even less noise.

Tielle strains to hear anything she can identify as an animal noise.

A third thud sounds, and silence falls.

"You may send the mist away, Lady Tielle," says a quiet, vibrant male voice. "Please summon an illumination scroll if you can."

"Gabriel?" Tielle calls.

"I'm all right." Gabriel's voice is strained but strong. "It's

Adaram Serco. He's a family friend."

Heart still racing, Tielle follows the instructions, closing her eyes to concentrate. Conjuring something is far easier than reversing the process, so she simply conjures the mist into the next room, which Lady Corabelle had assured her would be empty. Retrieving an illumination scroll, Tielle releases a single, bright energy orb from it.

A small man steps in front of her.

She's too weary to be embarrassed by this stranger seeing her in a nightdress.

"Please avert your gaze, my lady," says Adaram. He's dressed head-to-toe in a black form-fitting suit.

The dark clothes don't reveal much, but Tielle catches a brief glimpse of a bloody dagger before the man can send the weapon away.

Vic!

Ignoring the man, Tielle rushes past the bodies to reach the crib. She stops short when she spots Gabriel holding the crying baby. The sight causes her heartbeats to slow. Her gaze wanders left to the bodies, but Adaram blocks her view once more.

"Who were they?" she asks. "What did they want? Are there more?"

"I don't know two of them, but the leader may be an assassin and mercenary known as Barsi," answers Adaram with a frown. "He usually operates in Outreach. Master Marcus guessed that several high-end mercenaries would receive contracts on the child, but I'm not sure if he would have guessed somebody on Barsi's level."

"Will there be others?" Gabriel wonders.

"Likely not tonight," says Adaram. "I will speak with the house Minder, contact my master, and report to Lady Corabelle. Meanwhile, you should probably find a new room to rest in. I'm sure Master Marcus will send somebody to safeguard you tonight."

"I don't want my mother disturbed," says Gabriel.

"I'm guessing the Minder on duty already roused her." Adaram looks sympathetic. "All the more reason to set up elsewhere."

"We can use Jack's old room," says Gabriel. "It's right next to this one." He nods in the appropriate direction.

"I moved the mist there." Tielle tries not to sound defensive. "It should dissipate by morning, but it won't be comfortable for a few hours."

"Is there another suitable room?" asks Adaram.

Gabriel stiffens.

"Marina's," Tielle answers, picking up on her husband's discomfort. Moving to his side, she loops an arm through his elbow. "She would like the idea of her old room being a safe place for her daughter to rest. I can move the crib, and we can carry some blankets if the bed's not prepared."

"It is," says Lady Corabelle from near the door. "I had every guest room prepared once Daniel agreed to let Victoria stay with us."

"Your instincts proved accurate, my lady." Adaram bows to Gabriel's mother. "I must contact my master, but I will be nearby if you need me again."

"Where did you come from?" asks Gabriel.

Tielle picks up on the hard note in his tone.

With another bow, the small man leaves the room.

"I had him wait in Jackson's room," answers Lady Corabelle.

"You knew," Gabriel whispers, staring at his mother in horror.

Lady Corabelle's expression remains unreadable.

"I knew only what I still know," she answers evenly, "Victoria is in danger, and if those after her cannot find an opportunity, they will make one."

"She could have been killed!" Gabriel snaps. "My wife could have been killed!"

His shouts upset Vic who intensifies her cries.

Tielle tightens her grip on her husband's arm, trying to stop him before he says something regrettable.

It doesn't work.

"I could have been killed!" Gabriel shouts. "Did you consider that this plan could mean losing two children in less than a week?"

Tielle watches the question strike Lady Corabelle and sink in like a well-placed sword thrust.

"That's not fair, Gabriel," says Tielle, though her chest still aches from the lightning bolt. "Besides, the plan worked. We're alive and safe."

"Are we safe?" Gabriel directs the pointed question to his mother.

"For now," Lady Corabelle answers. "I can call some servants to deal with the bodies, and Marcus will send another Nokarti Assassin to replace Adaram. We can discuss what's to be done tomorrow. Get some rest."

Chapter 6:
The Dragon

Jackson's Camp, Forsaken Lands Region of the Badlands
One week after Marina's death
(Vic is still eight months old)

As he waits for the sleeping spells to release the four prisoners, Jackson builds a small stone pit and sets a magical fire for light and warmth. He looks around, but there's not much to see even in the daytime. The Badlands mainly feature cracked, red-brown clay covered with patchy areas of sand. Occasionally, a scrappy bush might grow, but like most other forms of life, plants abandoned these lands centuries ago. Moonlight gives Jackson a great view of the surrounding emptiness, but aside from keeping the prisoners calm, the fire will allow him to read the unfamiliar incantation off a scroll.

Something blocks the moonlight, but it's too brief to be a cloud.

Jackson's heart beats faster.

A challenging roar shatters the silence, causing the rocks Jackson placed over his scroll to tremble.

Do not fear the dragon. I have asked Malcorius to guard you tonight. He is announcing this to other creatures roaming the area.

"What other creatures?" Jackson wonders.

Dragons mostly, but there may be feral kitsarue or even rogue Denkari or common undead wandering about. They come here for the same reason that attracts you. The Darklands are close to this place.

"I thought the Denkari served you," says Jackson.

They did, and many still do. But even the most devoted soldiers grow weary when told to wait for generations. Some ask for—and are granted—permission to hunt to keep their skills sharp. Once in a while, a Denkari will overstay their leave. The time to bring them all to Aeris is coming. That is your purpose.

"Shouldn't I be seeking Victoria?" asks Jackson. "You said we must control her for Daniel to surrender the bracers."

He's barely begun his search, but I am tracking his progress. If he finds them, I will send you to fetch the child. Barsi's failure has made your family suspicious.

Poor Barsi. I didn't know my mother had those kinds of connections.

She does not, but Marcus Polani does. As for Barsi, he served his purpose. For a few days, your brother and his wife will be very alert, but they will let their guard down at some point. Your mother had the house wards lowered to set her trap. They are back in place, but you can come and go as you please. You have already proven that a small child can be safely conjured from place to place if they fit within your cloak.

Jackson spares a thought for the Bereft boy he dumped at an orphanage in Bastion.

I hope he's safe.

"What should I do with Victoria after we have the bracers?" Jackson's uncertain which way he wishes his master to answer. On the one hand, Victoria's death will negate Gabriel's importance as the child's sponsor, giving Jackson the opening to sue for control of the holdings. But it seems an unfair thing to do to his mother right now, so close to Marina's death.

Kill her.

"She's only a baby," Jackson argues. The memory of holding Victoria in Marina's apartment and then again at the Earth Temple Ruins comes to him unbidden. They had even spent some time watching the baby sleep before Marina foolishly threw her life away in a vain attempt to halt their plans.

She cannot be allowed to live. People are foolish. No matter what Victoria becomes, people will expect her to save them because of that silly prophecy. Crushed people fall faster. If we let them have hope—even irrational hope—they will be harder to conquer.

Jackson accepts this logic, mentally apologizing to his mother.

Your mother will recover from Victoria's death. It is kinder to strike this second blow close to the first, so she may mourn them together. I'm more concerned about the huntsman.

"Why? He's just a man."

He's a man shown great favor by the Lady of Light. My old rival could be terribly naïve and hopelessly optimistic, but she was rarely foolish. It would be great fun to turn him against the Lady and the Charlatan. I will ponder this. Are your prisoners awake yet?

"Soon, Master," Jackson assures the Dark Man.

A wall of wind knocks Jackson off his feet. He lands on his back near the fire. The intense heat doesn't bother him, but he rolls swiftly to his feet so he can defend himself. Another fierce wind slams into him, but he shifts his weight to weather the assault, lifting his cloak to protect his face from flying sand.

A tremendous roar followed by a resounding thump startles Jackson. He stares at his line of prisoners.

It's shorter by two.

A stream of dragon fire flashes across the sky, followed by another challenging roar.

It's answered by a bright blue streak and a different screech.

Frost dragon.

Prepare some fireballs. I will show you where to cast them.

Jackson braces for the discomfort that always accompanies the thrilling rush of energy as his master's spirit joins him. There's pain too, but he ignores it. Calling upon the Saroth Gift for fire, Jackson pulls the campfire remains to his hands and fashions it into a ball. This he hurls into the sky. Before he can consider where he's aiming, Jackson feels an irresistible compulsion to create another fireball. He does so. This one gets delivered slightly right of the last one.

Both explode with frightening force.

Jackson collapses, drained by the effort. The position gives him a spectacular view of the fight raging above.

Steam creates a cloud around the roiling pair. One dragon is pitch black. The other is brilliant blue with green scales and wings. They shriek and snarl, clawing at each other and releasing fire or ice, respectively, at each other. However, they're too close to do much damage. Their powerful wings buffet each other and send strong currents down at Jackson. He shields his eyes but continues to watch, too fascinated by the majestic creatures to be scared.

Stretch forth your hand.

Though the Dark Man never specifies which hand, Jackson instinctively raises his right hand toward the blue and green dragon. For a split-second, he feels the creature's lifeforce and draws the energy toward his body. The connection snaps, but it's enough. The frost dragon utters a frustrated cry as its reflexes slow. Seizing the opportunity, the black dragon blasts the frost dragon with fire. Sensing the kill, it cuts off the fire stream and darts forward, slamming into the smaller dragon.

The blue and green dragon's cry now holds pain.

Move.

Jackson rolls left twice, coughing on dust and sand.

The ground shakes as the two dragons slam into it. The resulting concussive force nearly bounces Jackson back to his feet. He lands on his hands and knees, staring.

The dragon pair stands no more than ten paces away from him, like a living statue. The black dragon's teeth are firmly locked around its foe's neck.

A whimper comes from the blue and green dragon.

Draw upon her lifeforce.

You want me to kill a dragon? Jackson's too stunned to voice the words.

It will not kill her, but she must be punished for stealing those intended for the role. Besides, this is the only option if you wish to proceed tonight.

Jackson realizes the spot the dragons landed is where he'd placed the prisoners. Two had been carried off and presumably consumed, but he can see at least one mangled arm sticking out from beneath the blue and green dragon's bulk.

Quickly.

Trembling with a combination of terror and thrill, Jackson walks over to the huddled dragons and places his right hand on the blue and green dragon's snout. Drawing in a lifeforce isn't new to him, but he's never tried this with a magical creature. Shapeshifters, certainly, but not dragons. Each experience unfolds differently. Most people feel like stepping into a gentle river current or basking in soft rain. The dragon's lifeforce slams into Jackson like a fierce summer storm. Without his master's spirit present, his body likely could not withstand the flow.

By the time Jackson pulls back his hand, he feels happy, content, and invincible.

The black dragon growls and releases the blue and green dragon's neck. She quickly backs up, snorts with disdain, and yowls a complaint, shaking her head violently. The black dragon barks an order, which the smaller dragon reluctantly heeds. Leaping into the sky, she flies away. The black dragon soon follows suit.

I will have him circle a little closer this time.

The Dark Man's spirit leaves, but Jackson's head still buzzes with raw magical energy. Knowing the euphoric feeling won't last, he rushes back to his firepit then searches for the scroll. Fortunately, the wind currents from the fight threw enough sand and rocks over the scroll to partially bury it instead of blowing it away. After brushing off the enchanted scroll, Jackson resets the four stones holding down the corners.

Casting a fireball toward the pit, Jackson adds a source of magic to the base to keep the flame lit until his ritual completes.

Muttering a basic spell to make reading the words easier, Jackson settles in to work. He starts by running the complicated words over in his mind a few times before giving them voice. The first phrases yield nothing, but by the time he reaches the middle of the spell, the air in front of him shimmers. As soon as he stops speaking, the effect disappears.

Do it again. You mispronounced two words.

Despite his fatigue, Jackson follows the command, taking special note of the two words the Dark Man highlights on the scroll. The reading spell lets the words flow through his mind without constantly referring to the text, so Jackson closes his eyes to concentrate on letting the words shape the magic within him. When the last word crosses his lips, Jackson opens his eyes.

A tall portal stands before him. Its borders resemble a mirror, but instead of reflective glass, it shows him a grim, dusty place. It looks devoid of animal life. He spots some trees and mountains in the distance, but he cannot see them clearly. Everything appears gray, like he's peering through smoke.

Knees weak from the effort, Jackson kneels before the portal. The surface shimmers. The borders flicker, then fade. The dusty, gray place vanishes from view.

Jackson groans.

Do not despair. You will improve.

But what did we accomplish?

You have proven a point. The Darklands are within reach. When the time comes to retrieve my armies from beyond this world, you will have the power to open and sustain many such

portals. Meanwhile, let us turn our thoughts to Daniel. Besides Victoria, not many people hold sway over his heart. That complicates matters. He is far from a committed ally, and once this business with Victoria completes, he will be a bitter enemy once more.

"What about the Arkonai woman?" asks Jackson. "You said she had a connection to Daniel."

Lady Christa, the one with the intriguing child.

"Would Daniel risk himself for her?"

Probably, but Jordan Lekros—the lady's husband—would hardly stand for that. For a man who publicly denies having a wife, he's completely obsessed with her. Several huntsmen have the sole job of informing Jordan every time the lady leaves Shadow Oaks. His jealousy may present a unique opportunity to grow the strife between Daniel and the Arkonai Hunting Guild, but I'm not yet sure if that benefits us.

"If we decided to move against Lady Christa, how would we get to her?" Jackson inquires. "We have no assets within Aridel."

I have some, but none within Lady Christa's household. Still, an asset may be cultivated easily enough with the proper bribe or threat. I could even send you in disguise as long as we do not need to move the prisoner.

"I've never been there," Jackson points out. "So, unless I can connect to something within the house, I won't be able to conjure myself into position."

Leave that to me. We must first decide what to do with the lady once we acquire her. Such a move will certainly cause a stir. That may have a wonderful destabilizing effect, but I'm still actively recruiting huntsmen. I'm not ready to destroy the Guild yet.

"What about poison?" asks Jackson, only half-listening to his master's musings. "If we find the right one, we could hold Lady Christa within our power from afar."

The Dark Man's laughter rolls through his mind.

A worthy thought. Go to one of your private retreats and rest. I will consult some other servants on your suggestion. Meanwhile, it is time you took a more active hand in protecting your niece. If they trust you, they will let you close to the child, then you can bring her to me.

Chapter 7:
Quest for the Magic Bracers

Somewhere in the Enchanted Forest
One week and one day after Marina's Death
(Vic is still eight months old)
Daniel already hates this quest. He'd spent half the week making arrangements for Vic, justifying his actions before the High Council, and searching through the Alamon Temple's extensive history collection. Then, once he'd determined the best starting place was within the Enchanted Forest, he'd spent yet more time waiting for the Tariku League to grant him permission to enter the forest and fending off propositions from treasure hunters who wanted to join him. To make matters worse, Huntmaster Taron's claim that there would be many false trails due to his Seeker Gifts behaving erratically once inside the forest proved accurate.

Let's hope Lady Gera's prediction of magical traps is wrong when we do find the bracers.

She's rarely wrong about such things.

"Cheery, Marcus. Thanks," Daniel mutters, resisting the urge to draw a dagger and stab the nearest tree.

Sorry. Good news first then. Katrina's using her puppy form to keep your daughter entertained, and there haven't been any other incidents.

Daniel tenses at the reference to the attack on Vic. He appreciates the care Lady Corabelle took in safeguarding his daughter, but he has very mixed feelings about using Vic as bait for the trap. Marcus's assurance that Adaram would not have let the would-be

43

kidnappers lay a finger on Vic helps, but Daniel's not pleased his daughter needs such ardent protection.

I'm about to lose the connection. Things are fine but find those bracers quickly. I believe my servants and soldiers would appreciate letting Lady Corabelle return to her own estate. She does *not* like being told what to do, and I believe Tielle grows weary of playing peacekeeper between her husband and his mother.

I can imagine, and you have my word to hurry.

Daniel waits for the connection to break before finishing his thoughts.

I'm not sure how much time Vic has.

Before returning to Aridel after Marina's burial, Kyle Ricci had examined Vic's hand and told Daniel that Marina's protection could last a while, but he could not guarantee a time beyond a few days. That many days had come and gone during preparations. Lady Corabelle had given Daniel a Teleportation scroll set for Dominance, but the Enchanted Forest had a well-known reputation for making magic go awry within its borders.

"They're close," says Raelyn.

Despite having heard these words many times today, Daniel feels his heart lift with hope. In truth, his own Gifts confirm the feeling. He pictures the many artistic and historical depictions of the magic bracers. It's the best he can do since nobody has laid eyes upon them in centuries. He feels foolish for even bothering. Some accounts describe the bracers as little more than oversized silver bracelets. Others show ornate, gaudy pieces of armor fit for a warrior king. Daniel wants to dismiss both images, but something about them rings true in his spirit.

"And now they're gone," Raelyn announces.

As Daniel opens his mouth to argue the point, his senses tell him she speaks truth. Unfortunately, this is a familiar frustration to them.

"Would you like a drink?" Daniel asks. Without waiting for an answer, he opens the Veil and withdraws a waterbag, grateful that part of his abilities still works. He would rather not consume anything from the forest. His eagerness to finish this quest battles his consideration for the Healer. It's also well past time for a break.

Raelyn shrugs and accepts the waterbag from him. After pausing to drink, she returns it with a nod of thanks before sitting on a fallen log and closing her eyes to concentrate.

Daniel wants to ask her how she's searching for the bracers

without Seeker Gifts, but aside from not wanting to offend her, he's not certain he wishes to hear if the answer has anything to do with the Dark Man. He hasn't forgotten that the malevolent spirit killed his wife and wounded his daughter to set him on this path. The thought causes a burning sensation to flare up in his chest.

"Peace, Daniel. Hatred's not a path you wish to walk," says Raelyn.

Not wanting to debate, Daniel merely grunts to acknowledge the statement.

This would go faster teleporting.

He dismisses the idea. It's dangerous with his Gifts this unpredictable, and Raelyn would not be able to follow.

"Pray with me," says Raelyn.

"Why?" The question flies out of Daniel. Restless energy causes him to walk away a few paces before facing the Healer again. Though he's known her for several years, Daniel has never given much thought to Raelyn's beliefs. Throughout the entire history of his acquaintance with her, she was just Marina's apprentice.

"Because what we seek belongs to the Lady, and we won't reach them without her blessing," Raelyn answers. Her breath sounds labored. She shifts over on the log. "We may as well formally present our requests."

Resigning himself to a few more minutes of rest, Daniel draws near. Noticing her flushed cheeks and sheen of sweat, he halts and kneels before the fair-haired woman.

"Are you all right?"

"For now," she answers, managing a weak smile.

The large black stone attached to a thin, leather strap glints in the light.

"It's that thing," Daniel declares, glaring at the evil object. His hand lifts, wanting to snatch the pendant off her neck and cast it into the woods.

Raelyn catches his hand. Her sleeve slips down enough to show the angry red line encircling her wrist.

"There's too much light in the forest for him to bear," she explains, releasing Daniel's hand. "He's not happy about that, but take heart, we will succeed this day. Will you let me pray?"

Resting his hands on his legs, Daniel maintains the kneeling position and bows his head.

Raelyn's hands land upon his shoulders.

"Holy and Eternal King, grant us favor with your servant, the Lady of Light. We are told only the worthy may command the bracers, but none who walk this land are worthy. Only you can cleanse us of the corruption that springs from our souls. Clear our minds and reveal the means of saving Daniel's daughter."

Daniel's spirit drinks in the words like refreshing spring water. The prayer surprises him because most Arkonai are taught to pray directly to the Lady of Light on the assumption that many needs can be addressed by Kailon's trusted, immortal servant.

As Daniel regains his feet, young Shadow comes to mind. *Devin.*

"I need to check something," Daniel says. "Will you be—"

"Go," Raelyn commands. This time, her smile contains genuine warmth. "Seek your answers. I will be waiting."

Not caring which direction his power takes him, Daniel teleports toward the edge of the Enchanted Forest.

"Marcus." Daniel repeats the call several times.

Two connections in one afternoon. To what do I owe the pleasure, Master Seeker?

I need you to map my mind. Where have we been today?

He experiences increased pressure on his head as his Minder friend works.

I apologize for the discomfort.

Just get me that map.

It's done. Explain later.

Thanking his friend for the understanding and brevity, Daniel teleports back to Raelyn. It takes him two tries to accomplish the task, stretching his Gifts tremendously. He staggers until Raelyn touches his left arm and heals the intense headache brought on by the overexertion.

"I know how to find the bracers," says Daniel, "but I need your help."

"You have it," Raelyn promises. Concern flavors her tone. "But you should rest a few hours."

Daniel shakes his head.

"Vic may not have that long."

A sad look comes over Raelyn.

"Very well. What do you need me to do?"

"We've been walking for hours, seemingly at random, but there's a pattern," Daniel explains. "Every time we get close, the bracers disappear. It's similar to my last hunt. The boy I pursued had a Seeker's ability to teleport. Every time he got scared, he would spontaneously use that ability. I need you to walk fifty paces in this direction." Daniel adjusts his body and points in the correct direction. "Meanwhile, I will wait at the next point along the trail."

The crude plan succeeds on their fourth try. Daniel has never accomplished so many teleports in a row without rest, but he doesn't question the good fortune, attributing the oddity to a quirk of the forest.

The bracers land in Daniel's hands. They're two thin silver bracelets, only slightly different than one of the artist's illustrations. One not accustomed to sensing magic would easily dismiss the pair as trinkets.

Daniel vanishes from the Enchanted Forest and appears deep in a mountain cave.

Evil surrounds him, making the cool air difficult to breathe.

"Put the bracers on!" calls Raelyn.

"Silence!" barks the Dark Man.

Raelyn yelps.

Daniel spins toward the voices, desperately wishing he could control fire like a Saroth.

Several torches lining the cave ignite simultaneously, revealing a grim scene.

Raelyn stands several paces away, bound by living shadows. They anchor her feet, wind up her legs, bind her hands together near her waist, and encompass her chest and neck. The red marks along both wrists glow brighter, shining through the shadows.

"Claim the bracers!" Raelyn orders, clearly fighting for the words.

"Surrender them or she dies," hisses the Dark Man. This time, he uses the body of a Bereft teenager. The deep voice doesn't fit the innocent face.

The impossible choice crushes Daniel. Every instinct tells him he needs the bracers to save his daughter, but he cannot sacrifice another life to accomplish the goal.

Fear not, Daniel. Raelyn is beyond his reach. She has been this whole time.

The voice filling his head belongs to the Lady.

Daniel locks eyes with Raelyn.

She nods solemnly, closes her eyes, and slumps against the shadows.

The shadows release Raelyn, dropping to the ground like discarded cords before vanishing.

Quickly, Daniel slips a silver bracelet onto each of his wrists.

Screeching, the teen corpse charges into Daniel, plucks him up like a child, and drives his back into the nearest cave wall.

A bright white light flashes.

Daniel feels the impact as his back meets the wall, but it doesn't bother him. Perfect peace surrounds and indwells him.

The Dark Man retreats and looks down at his smoking hands. The corpse's blank eyes glow red. He pins Daniel in place with a malevolent look but makes no further move to physically harm him.

"Foolish decision," declares the Dark Man. "Last chance to surrender the bracers. I'll even save your daughter as a reward."

Daniel detects the lie and rejects it. Knowledge floods him.

"You fear Vic," he says. "Who she is. What she'll become."

"I fear nothing." The Dark Man's voice rumbles with anger. "Your defiance will lead to many deaths, starting with your daughter and your dear friend, Christa. Every pain they suffer will be your fault. Neither you nor they will ever know peace again."

He cannot know the future.

Once more, the Lady's voice floats through Daniel's mind, but her comfort can only drive off some of the chill the threats inject into his soul.

The bracers are my gift to the world, a tool to fight the coming darkness. Use them well or grant their power to another. The choice is yours.

Daniel's heart aches as he crouches by Raelyn's body.

"What happened to her?"

She crossed over into the Darklands the same night Marina did. I met her there by chance. Her last prayer was to return long enough to aid you. Seeing the selflessness of this request, I agreed to make it so, though I made clear it would not be easy. She affirmed her choice, so I let her return for a time by staying with her.

Everything about the changes in Raelyn suddenly makes sense.

"Will you help me take her home?"

My powers have limits, but I can get you to the Enchanted Forest and help you bury her. Please remove the soulstone from her neck. That should remain here, hopefully never to be found again.

Chapter 8:
Grace Freely Given

North Library, Polani Estate, City of Jorash
One week and one day after Marina's death
(Vic is still eight months old)
Tielle Castaloni.

The thought brings Tielle on another strange tour of emotions. Joy, sorrow, regret, and love tumble around in her gut. The combined effect leaves her weary. She had spent much of her teenage years mourning the impossibility of ever marrying the man she loved.

About two weeks ago, she'd learned her dreams would become reality when Gabriel officially proposed. She would have married him that day, but his mother said a long engagement would let them design and prepare their own estate at her expense. Though disappointed at the delay, the offer thrilled them. Even with Gabriel's generous income from the holdings, they wouldn't have been able to afford their own estate for years.

Tielle had drawn comfort from the fact that the arrangement let her continue watching Vic for Marina as needed and otherwise helping Gabriel with his duties. Lady Corabelle had insisted Tielle spend several months being tutored in the history of the noble houses. The move didn't surprise her because a similar scenario unfolded with Gabriella before her marriage to Marcus. Given Tielle's love of history, it would have been delightful to take in the new information. Her new position greatly expands the scope of things she must learn, including Arkonai and Bereft culture and customs. If she could change the past, she would gladly return to her lower station.

Two weeks. So much change. So much heartache.

Vic screeches.

Katrina barks, bounds to the far side of the room, whirls three times, and dashes back.

Tielle leaps up and gasps as the puppy barrels into Vic, sending her sprawling.

Hysterical laughter and excited barks fill the room.

The little ones have done this to her numerous times tonight, but it still has the power to steal her breath. The first time, she had swooped in and examined Vic from every side. Katrina used the time to flip from puppy form to beetle to human multiple times. Having grown up with a Shapeshifter best friend, the activity didn't faze Tielle. Discovering no harm done to Vic, she had waited for Katrina to take human form before scooping her up for inspection. Since then, her observations have been more cursory.

Sinking back onto the couch, Tielle continues her musings of recent life changes. She'd gone from being engaged to a ridiculously handsome, humble, perfect man to becoming his wife. She'd lost the woman she most admired in the world before really getting to know her. The occasional fun, chaotic duty of watching a precious baby girl turned into a terrifying, semi-permanent situation.

The day has stretched on forever. Even with Gabriel by her side and guards in the halls, Tielle could only sleep fitfully. She thought morning might ease her, but the chaos of moving to the Polani estate drained her energy faster than waiting at the Castaloni estate. First Marcus, then Gabriel, and finally, Lady Corabelle left to attend other business.

The midday meal occupied some time. Intermittent naps for the little ones consumed part of the afternoon. A light evening meal passed pleasantly but slowly.

Jackson appears near the door, far to Tielle's right.

Her first clue to the change comes from Katrina. Still in puppy form, she plants her body in front of Vic. Black fur along her back stands on edge. She crouches low, tucks her tail between her legs, and growls.

Overcoming her fear, Tielle dives for Vic. The baby shrieks and laughs like it's a game. The impulse to shove Vic behind her and clutch her close collide, leaving Tielle with her body half-twisted away from Jackson.

"My apologies for the intrusion," he says.

"Who are you?" demands a man materializing behind Jackson.

He holds a dagger but does not raise it.

Shapeshifter.

Marcus had warned Tielle some guards wouldn't make their presence known unless absolutely necessary.

"Hold," calls another guard, entering from the hallway. "It's Jackson Castaloni. He's on the approved list. Remember? The Conjurer."

The first guard slips his dagger away, backs up a step, bows, and mumbles an apology.

"Lady Corabelle is not here, my lord," says the hallway guard, "but she said you might inquire about her. Master Marcus arranged for her to have an office at the Academy of Arts and Sciences."

"Thank you, but I also came to check on my niece." Jackson's tone conveys mild amusement and studied boredom.

With another bow, the guards return to their posts. The Shapeshifter becomes a mouse and slips under the door after it closes.

"She's fine," Tielle says coldly. The fading sense of danger leaves room for anger. She settles into a more comfortable position where she can hold Vic and soothe the puppy. "What were you thinking? Didn't you hear what happened?"

"What do you think brought me here?" Jackson returns.

"The last people who appeared unannounced are dead." Tielle tries valiantly to keep her voice steady. "Send a messenger or use a Minder next time."

"I did not realize I had frightened you so." Jackson sounds apologetic, but his eyes mock her.

Not liking her confinement, Vic wriggles and whines, babbling a protest.

"It has been a trying day," Tielle admits, trying to sort her muddled feelings.

Aside from the attack meant to intimidate Gabriel eons ago, she's had little to do with Jackson. Her husband might be won over by the man's apparent change of heart, but something about him makes her wary. The magic currents around him feel tainted. As a Conjurer, she knows the advanced levels of the art can take one to some dark places, but she has nothing more than a feeling to prove Jackson's studies have progressed that far.

He's your brother in the eyes of Saroth law. Try to love him, or at least pretend to tolerate him better.

"I shall take my leave then," says Jackson, disappearing before

Tielle can respond.

Katrina relaxes and barks a message Tielle imagines as *good riddance.*

The children return to their games.

Too tired to move, Tielle stays on the plush carpet, watching a wrestling match turn into a strange form of tag. Vic may not be able to walk yet, but she can cover a lot of ground with a crawl. Recognizing the baby's limits, the toddler stays in puppy form, ducking and dodging more than outright dashing away. Their endless energy amazes Tielle.

For safety reasons, this inner library has been transformed into a playroom with an illusion of sunny windows along the east wall. The artificial beams feel as warm as real ones.

As a pleasant feeling sets in, the door bursts open and two different guards enter with a prisoner.

Tielle sits bolt upright.

"Da!" Vic cries.

A pang pierces Tielle's heart. She blinks at the child.

Shock and awe cover Daniel's face too, but there's no time to celebrate Vic's first coherent word.

Tielle scrambles to her feet.

Katrina takes her human form and sits cross-legged on the floor, watching as if having armed men enter a room is normal.

Considering Marcus's occupation, it may be normal.

"This Arkonai demanded entrance," reports the taller guard. "We told him he'd have to wait for Master Marcus to return in a few hours, but he would not be persuaded."

"Don't worry, my lady. He's under a confinement spell," adds the other guard. "He can't hurt you."

Before Tielle can stop her, Vic darts forward until she smacks into the confinement spell surrounding Daniel. Frustrated and confused, she cries.

"Da!" Vic pounds a tiny fist into the strangely solid air.

As a puppy, Katrina whines sympathetically and nudges the child away from the magic barrier.

Gaining a few wits back, Tielle picks up both children.

"Release him." Though meant to be an order, Tielle's words barely qualify as a whisper.

"I can't do that until I receive orders from the master of the house," says the first guard.

"Then get him." This second order has more snap to it. Tielle simultaneously wants to hug Daniel and weep.

"He's in a meeting," says the shorter guard.

"Don't you think he'd want to know his friend has returned from an important quest?" Tielle argues.

The guards merely repeat earlier sentiments.

"Why isn't he speaking?" Tielle wonders, feeling faint at the strangeness. Her arms ache from holding the children, forcing her to set them down.

They return to the barrier.

Daniel tries to smile and gestures the best he can with bound hands. Though clumsy, the request for patience and calm is clear. Kneeling, he waves to Vic.

"The huntsman gave his word not to speak until released from the confinement," explains the first guard.

Tielle studies Daniel as he makes faces to entertain Vic. His beige pants, brown boots, tan shirt, and leather vest bear dirt and sweat stains. The bindings around his wrists look tight, but he doesn't seem anxious.

Spotting the silver bracelets Daniel wears above the wrist restraints, Tielle shoots him a significant look.

He beams.

"May I at least give him a stool?" Tielle asks.

The guards exchange looks, then nod.

The effort takes a lot out of Tielle, but she eventually conjures a stool for Daniel to perch on.

"Where is the house Minder?" Tielle demands.

Neither guard can answer her since they are not part of the house.

I must reach Marcus.

Tielle's attention falls on Katrina. The child's deep green eyes stare back, giving Tielle an idea.

"Katrina, can you find your father?"

The child nods slowly.

"Show me, please," says Tielle, picking up Vic. "We'll be right back." She aims the statement at Daniel. "Hopefully with Marcus."

Once again in puppy form, Katrina barks happily and trots out of the room. Tielle follows with Vic. They locate the Minder within minutes, but it takes well over an hour for Tielle to explain the situation, the Minder to get a message to somebody who can contact Marcus, and for him to hurry home.

Upon returning to the North Library, Tielle renews the plea to release Daniel, but the guards consistently refuse, claiming a prior incident.

Daniel only shrugs.

Accepting his calm as a good sign, Tielle spends the rest of the time entertaining Vic and Katrina.

Marcus's arrival heralds excellent things. He signs for custody of Daniel, forces the guards to break the confinement spell, and has the guards escorted out before embracing his friend.

Impatient, Vic and Katrina interrupt.

Katrina barks for her father's attention.

"I didn't forget you, Kat," says Marcus. He bends down and plucks her off the floor. By the time he brings her up to his chest, she's in human form with arms flung wide for a hug.

At the same time, Vic crawls over to her father's leg and uses his boot to hoist herself to a standing position. A second later, she lands on her butt and starts crying, but that doesn't detract from the accomplishment.

Daniel sweeps Vic up into his arms and holds her close.

Tielle blinks back tears, sparing a second to wish Marina could witness the changes in Vic.

"Will you hold her?" Daniel asks, looking at Tielle.

Not sure she has the strength to do this standing, Tielle settles onto the floor. Daniel deposits Vic into her waiting arms. After a quick hug and kiss, Tielle turns Vic around so she faces her father.

Vic mumbles something random.

Daniel kneels.

For her part, Vic goes completely still.

Slowly, Daniel pulls the silver bracelets off his wrists, first the left and then the right.

Tielle stares hard at his arms. All traces of irritation from the chains have disappeared.

"Hold out her hands," Daniel instructs.

Tielle complies, gripping Vic's elbows and lifting the child's hands toward Daniel. The baby's left hand and arm bear perfectly normal flesh. In contrast, the right arm looks normal, but everything from her wrist down to her tiny fingertips is cool, dead flesh. It reminds Tielle of the magical wound Marina sustained years ago and bore to her dying day.

"Vic, the Lady of Light has given me a sign of her grace this day," says Daniel. "What was given freely, I now pass on for the preservation of your life. Wear these magic bracers always. They will protect you even when I cannot."

With that, he slips the giant bracelets onto Vic's skinny wrists.

To Tielle's astonishment, the bracelets shrink and elongate until they form miniature bracers, filling the space between Vic's elbows and wrists.

Vic laughs and claps her hands.

The bracers flash, releasing a burst of magic.

Alarmed, Tielle and Daniel search Vic for injury but find nothing different. Her arms look the same, as do her hands, feet, and precious face. Nevertheless, Tielle feels the difference. Something dark and oppressive has left the child.

"Why isn't her hand healed?" Daniel asks.

Tielle opens her mouth to admit not having an answer, but a woman's ageless, calming voice speaks within her mind.

Some corruptions take longer to heal, and some Gifts are meant for certain times. Victoria will live, but what she will become is known only to the One.

Chapter 9:
Two Bargains

Shadow Oaks, Home of Lady Christa, City of Aridel
Ten months after Marina's death
(Vic is a year and a half old; Christa's twins are about seven and a half years old)

Jackson appears in the child's room as planned, hoping the information he paid dearly for proved accurate. Hunting down traitors could be fun, but this venture had already stretched on far longer than anticipated. He knew infiltrating an estate inside Aridel's vaunted First Ring would be difficult, but he'd underestimated the loyalty of Lady Christa's servants. It had taken him ten months of secret meetings, creative threats, and hard work to plan this night.

Do not kill the child. She has discovered Seeker Gifts recently. It's a late manifestation for Arkonai youths, but I have felt the latent potency of her power. She is but a child now, but it will not always be so. Given a decade or more to grow and train, and she may become a powerful ally. Nevertheless, you must be convincing, or the lady will not yield.

After applying the sleep scroll to the girl, Jackson releases three energy orbs from an illumination scroll and tucks the spent parchment into his unfamiliar belt. He had considered merely using fireballs, as he likes the warmer glow of their light, but his master insisted he do nothing uniquely Saroth tonight. Though not the first time wearing Arkonai clothing, Jackson finds the pants, shirt, and vest confining.

Stop fidgeting. She will be here shortly. You must exude confidence.

"Should I threaten the girl now?" Jackson wonders, touching the dagger's hilt. It's strange to have the sheath attached to a belt and not tucked into his robes.

Not yet. The action will have more power if witnessed. Do not forget to alter your speech patterns accordingly.

Jackson understands the reminder to be a manifestation of his master's nervousness concerning the plan, but he's smart enough not to point that out. Instead, he sets up a privacy spell and uses a transformation scroll to temporarily alter his appearance. Though he typically doesn't bother checking the specifics, he notices that the spell should significantly lighten his dark hair and make his eyes appear blue. He paces around in a confident stride he's seen many Arkonai men employ.

The lady has arrived. Move into position.

The bedroom door swings open.

Jackson conjures himself into the correct position behind the door since the other option involves sprinting.

As the lady turns to close the door, Jackson calmly helps her with the task.

Uttering a small, surprised cry, she stumbles back two steps.

"Scream as you like," says Jackson, tailoring his voice to mimic an Arkonai accent. "Afterwards, we need to talk."

The woman backs up further, whirls, and checks on the child. After confirming that the girl sleeps soundly, the woman turns again and deliberately places herself between Jackson and the child.

The distance allows him to admire her. Lady Christa wears a lavender dress with an elegant silver pattern running from the shoulders across the bust and down the front before splitting along two new seams down the skirt. The normal part of her sleeves stop midway down the upper portion of her arms before flipping to a transparent, silky piece that flows well past her hands. The effect is undeniably beautiful and terribly impractical.

A dozen questions fly out at him from her eyes, but she holds them in and watches him carefully, arms spread away from her sides in a subtle, protective gesture.

The initial panic is past. You may proceed with the proposal.

"You're not a huntsman," says Lady Christa. "Your boots are too clean."

A chuckle rolls through Jackson's head, and his chest warms with his master's amusement.

The privacy spell is in place. You may drop the charade if you wish. There are enough markers to present the case we wish. It may even suit our purposes to have the deed blamed on your people.

Jackson straightens as he breaks the spell altering his features and allows the lady a long look at his dark hair and deep green eyes.

"Are you surprised to find a Saroth before you, Lady Christa?" Jackson asks, using his natural voice.

"I'm surprised to find anybody before me at this hour," says Lady Christa. "What brings you to Aridel?"

"You, of course," Jackson replies. "And your daughter."

The lady confines her surprise and alarm to a widening of her lovely gray-green eyes, but Jackson does not need the confirmation. He raises a hand to wave off pointless denials.

"Let us not waste time with idle chatter about how I know what I know," says Jackson. "Instead, allow me to explain your instructions." No longer bothering with pretense, Jackson conjures the vial of poison and holds it out for the lady to see. "You're going to drink this and return to your room before it takes full effect."

"What is it? What's it going to do to me?" Lady Christa inquires.

"Those answers are less important than what I'm going to do to your child if you refuse," Jackson answers. A snap of his fingers sends the vial away and has it reappear next to the lady. "To be blunt, I will kill her with this." He touches the dagger sheath.

The woman grips the vial hard, causing the bright green liquid inside to slosh around. The liquid would have been clear except the potions master added a dye to make it visible from afar.

Jackson reads Lady Christa's plan in the determined lines of her face.

"The glass container is very hearty," he comments, "and I have more." That part is a lie, so he prepares his powers should he need to rescue the vial from the Arkonai woman.

"What do I get in return?" inquires the lady.

"The life of your child," says Jackson. "I thought that part was clear enough."

"If you know about her, then you also know secrecy is a part of her safety," says Lady Christa. "Swear by the One to never reveal her identity to another living soul." Her eyes drift down to the vial nestled in her right hand. "And I will do as you say."

Make the deal. If I need the information to come out later, I have other servants to accomplish it.

Accepting the term, Jackson enters the binding verbal contract, knowing it will be backed up by magic. He may remember the thing he swears not to reveal, but like a fact uttered behind a privacy spell, he won't be able to discuss it, even once other forms of protections fade. The detail might have been covered by the privacy spell he put in place for their conversation, but since he controls that spell, Jackson cannot be certain. It's a small enough concession to purchase cooperation anyway.

"How quickly will this work?" asks Lady Christa.

"A few minutes," Jackson answers. "You should be able to retire to your own bedchamber. Don't worry about informing anybody, I will take care of that."

Sitting on the bed, the woman moves the vial to her other hand and rests her free hand on the girl's left cheek. The woman's head bows, but her voice is surprisingly strong as she speaks again.

"Am I to die?"

"That depends on the actions of others," Jackson answers honestly. "I have a counteragent for the poison, and a reason for forcing your hand."

Standing, Lady Christa leans over and kisses the girl before facing Jackson again.

"I need one more assurance," the lady announces.

"I grow short of patience, but continue," says Jackson.

"Tell me it's enough." Her expression turns troubled, and she blinks back tears.

She seeks to know you will not harm the child or anybody else in her household after she obeys the command to drink the poison.

Grateful for his master's explanation, Jackson answers the woman's concerns.

"If the potions master did his job correctly, it will be enough." Seeing that the answer doesn't quite satisfy her, he continues, "You may or may not lose consciousness from the poison, but it will weaken you greatly. The privacy spell will protect my identity but try not to speak on the matter at all. If my plan goes well, I will eventually return with the counteragent. If it does not, I may vent my frustrations on your house."

"Who are you trying to hurt?" asks the lady.

Do not answer that.

"I believe I have answered enough questions." Jackson grips the dagger's hilt. "Please fulfill your side of this bargain."

With one more glance back at the child, Lady Christa carefully pulls out the cork and lifts the vial to her lips. She hesitates, draws a bracing breath, closes her eyes, and drinks the green liquid. The warning that the brew might be bitter runs through Jackson's mind as he watches the lady's face. She winces but swallows the substance before slowly replacing the cork.

"Do you wish to take this?" she asks, holding up the glass vial.

"Please."

Lady Christa tosses him the container and takes three steps toward the door.

"Will you accompany me?"

Jackson's heart jumps at the strange request.

She wants you away from her daughter.

Not caring what her reasons may be, Jackson takes the lady's elbow and escorts her away from the servants' quarters up toward the larger bedrooms. He leaves her at the door to her bedchamber and moves on to his second meeting for the night. As soon as he appears in the Supreme Huntmaster's private gardens, his master delivers new instructions.

Dispense with the disguise. I believe you should meet Jordan Lekros as yourself. He will not arrive for another half-hour or so anyway. The business in Aridel took less time than anticipated.

Not sure what he thinks about the idea, Jackson stops in Fort Medron long enough to change into proper robes. Once back in the gardens, he spends the waiting time wandering the paths and visiting various fountains. He considers renewing the privacy spell, but his master assures him nobody will bother him or Seek to read these paths.

This is the Supreme Huntmaster's private sanctuary. We are here to prove a point. Downplay your significance. Tonight, you are simply my messenger. Remind him how much he has already gained from my benevolence and what he will lose if he stands against me.

You really want me to do this as me?

Yes. Let him believe it's a sign of my trust in him. Men like Jordan need to feel some control, or they lash out.

"Who are you and what brings you to my gardens?" demands Jordan Lekros. "And why shouldn't I summon my Pirok Guards?"

Be respectful yet firm.

Jackson bows deeply.

"My master sends his greetings, Supreme Huntmaster. As a sign of good faith, I shall answer your questions to the best of my abilities. My name is Jackson Castaloni. You have met my late sister, Marina."

"Did you kill her?" asks Jordan.

Deny that. He knows nothing.

"We are not here to discuss me," Jackson answers. "You have benefitted from my master's plans many times. He now requires something of you." As briefly as possible, Jackson walks the Supreme Huntmaster through some of the many times the Dark Man has worked things out in his favor. "You already owe the Master your position, your wealth, and even your life. He now extends the invitation to serve him in an even greater capacity."

If he gets stubborn, I will flood your mind with what to say and how to say it.

"What happens if I refuse?" Jordan inquires.

"Lady Christa dies."

Jackson watches as the Arkonai man's features cycle several emotions. Shock quickly gives way to anger which flips to defiance, uncertainty, and fear before settling on a duller form of grim surprise.

"But I—"

Righteous anger flashes through Jackson.

"Your foolish vows mean nothing! Denials do not change facts. You love her, and you are bound to her fate. Lady Christa has already taken a powerful poison this night. If she does not receive the counteragent within two weeks, she will die." Jackson feels drained as the speech ends. He silently watches the other man as his master speaks.

I am your master, Jordan. I can be a kind master or a cruel one. How I deal with you in the future depends on your actions now. I require two things of you. Send Daniel Saveron into the Enchanted Forest for at least two weeks, then bring me his daughter. Jackson will tell you where to deliver her when the time comes.

A lingering silence plus occasional nods from Jordan tells Jackson that the Dark Man is still speaking to him. Finally, the Supreme Huntmaster gives his response.

"Yes, Master."

He does not mean that yet, but he will one day. I will monitor the plan and remind him of his duties as necessary.

Chapter 10:
Arrest

Somewhere in the Enchanted Forest
Three days later (About ten months after Marina's death)
(Vic is a year and a half old; Christa's twins are about seven and a half years old)

Daniel scans his surroundings, trying to decide whether he wants to hunker down, keep moving, or climb a tree. Elias and Medris are both fair trackers, but their Seeker Gifts haven't developed much since he had worked with them over a year ago. He's surprised Jordan and the High Council consider them ready for an Ascension Trial. If they succeed, they will earn the right to be called huntsmen, officially join the Guild, and accept jobs. If they fail, they will train another six months and apply for a new test.

Electing to keep walking, Daniel selects a path through some dense underbrush. He's careful to keep signs of his presence at a minimum, but every branch he moves past should absorb a trace of him, leaving a trail for his pursuers. Moderately skilled Seekers can mask such traces, but Daniel wants to be found. This hunt has already stretched into a third day. He may have to leave more blatant signs if he wants to quit this strange forest and return to his daughter.

The thought of Vic distracts him. Normally, Daniel would force himself to focus, but since the distraction might aid him in leaving a better trail for the apprentices to follow, he lets his thoughts linger.

She's changed so much.

Instead of crawling everywhere, Vic's now running and crashing everywhere. She also says *no* a lot, screeches at impressive volumes, and has several teeth. Tielle even reported that Vic started showing an interest in chamber pots and outhouses.

Daniel sends the One silent thanks for Tielle. He's not sure how he and Vic would have survived the months since Marina's death without her. Any day Daniel needs childcare, he arranges for Tielle to meet him at the portal in Dominance.

As the trees open into a clearing leading to a stream, Daniel presses a palm against the nearest tree to leave a better mark for the apprentices to track. Recognizing the area, Daniel realizes he's close to Raelyn's grave. The desire to visit meets the painful memory of bringing her parents and her brother to the site. At the time, he had managed to remain stoic, but the young woman's loss hurts even more because Marina had fought so hard to save her. The Lady had confirmed Raelyn's account of Marina's work to save her from the soulstone, though she could add nothing more to the tale.

Knowing he will regret missing the opportunity, Daniel masks his mark and picks a path across the shallow stream to the tranquil location the Lady had selected for Raelyn's resting place. For some reason, he doesn't want the apprentices to find the grave. Sitting beside the smooth stone marker, Daniel rests his hand atop the stone.

Your work lives on.

He means the words for Marina and Raelyn, though both are far beyond caring. It helps to know they would both appreciate the gesture. He's speaking of the Heart and Hope Center in Temperance. Marina had established the original healing clinic in the neutral city, but hatred had consumed the first building in an attack meant to drive Marina out of Temperance. She had willingly turned the restoration efforts over to Raelyn Cordova and the young Healer's father, Emeric.

"Your father agreed to continue running the clinic until a permanent replacement can be found," Daniel reports, "but I think he may stay on and continue overseeing the work himself, especially if he can convince your brother to move down from Aridel and help. Regardless, the place will have the funds to continue healing efforts for many years. Marina would never forgive me if I let the work stop simply because she's gone."

After a few more minutes updating Raelyn on Vic's latest adventures, Daniel gets up, crosses the stream again, stops masking his mark, and continues his hike through the Enchanted Forest. Being close to the forest's edge tempts Daniel to check in with Marcus. He can almost imagine his friend begging him to reach out, but that's likely wishful thinking since he's the one missing his daughter terribly.

This is the longest we've been apart in months.

Since Marina's death, Daniel has only accepted short, easy jobs from the Guild. He wouldn't have even agreed to this one except Jordan had argued the point so strongly. Daniel would rather spend his days watching Vic, checking in on one of the charities, or training with Marcus's soldiers and spies. He'd built Katrina and Vic a small army of wooden animals and thought maybe he would build more for some of the orphanages in Bastion and Aridel. With his current expenses, he could get by taking very few jobs a year, less if he accepted money from the Castalonis for Vic's care.

What should I do, Marina?

Daniel shakes his head, wondering if it's still acceptable for him to be addressing questions to his dead wife. He could ask Marcus, but he already knows the Minder's answer. Vic deserves the chance to make her own choice on her mother's legacy, but the training to run the Castaloni holdings will take her away from him for many years. The position itself comes with many stresses and dangers Daniel would never willingly subject an enemy to, let alone his baby girl.

A distant rustling sound catches Daniel's attention. He freezes and casts his senses into the nearby area, noting the presence of hundreds of insects and dozens of small creatures. A deer bounds away with loud crashing noises. Daniel waits to see if the disturbance will draw one of the apprentices, but he eventually loses hope of that happening when the wildlife returns to its normal rhythms.

Another impulse to call Marcus washes over Daniel. This one feels slightly different.

What if I'm not imagining things? What if something's wrong with Vic?

A significant use of his Gifts could give away his position, but he could mask his mark again before teleporting. The Dark Man had made no moves against Vic, Christa, or Marina's family, but he would eventually. Since Daniel has no way of predicting the evil spirit's next move, he must remain vigilant.

When yet another urge to check on his daughter enters his mind, Daniel teleports to the forest's edge.

Daniel!

Marcus's call booms inside Daniel's head, loud enough to reverberate in his chest. He hasn't heard Marcus this frantic in a long time. To Daniel's surprise, another Minder reaches out to him.

Master Daniel, this is Navina Christol. Please contact

Master Marcus soon.

I'm here.

Lacking Minder Gifts, Daniel cannot reach out to connect to either mind, but Gabriella and Marcus had taught him how to think loudly enough to call them.

Thank you, Navina. I can give him the message.

Daniel doesn't hear the other Minder's response, but a faint pressure lifts off his head, announcing her exit from the conversation.

What message?

Though he tries to contain his dread, Daniel recognizes the grim flavor of his friend's thoughts.

Two beats of silence pass.

A while ago, you asked me to check in on Lady Christa Lekros.

"Out with it, Marcus," Daniel orders.

She has been poisoned.

Daniel's mind fires the standard barrage of questions about how and when it happened, why Christa, and how she fares.

Nobody knows how or why for sure, but rumors point to Saroth involvement. Healers have said she's stable but unconscious. The Tariku League requests that you investigate on their behalf.

"I will leave at once," Daniel promises. "Give me a moment to collect the two apprentices. I'll need to escort them to Bastion. I can get permission for the investigation from Jordan while I'm there."

It might be better to go directly to Aridel without talking to the Council. Formal requests for a meeting have been repeatedly rebuffed. Tensions are rising rapidly, and we don't know why.

"I need to enter the Enchanted Forest to collect the apprentices, so we're going to lose the connection," Daniel warns, "but I will update you when I can. Kiss Vic for me."

Of course. Be careful. Something's not right.

With Marcus's warning still fading from his mind, Daniel steps back inside the forest. Closing his eyes, he magnifies his Seeker presence to attract the apprentices' attention. When that fails, Daniel uses his Gifts to locate the pair. Elias is somewhere southwest of his position while Medris is near the forest's northern edge. Leaving the connection open, Daniel hopes at least one of them will teleport to him because he doesn't think his body can handle two long jumps right now.

Neither apprentice detects his blatant signal.

Praying his strength holds, Daniel jumps first to Elias's position and explains the situation. Next, they jump together to Medris's location and repeat the summary. Daniel instructs both young men to teleport to Bastion. They complain until reminded that a woman's life outweighs their Ascension Trial. From their frowns, Daniel gathers he has not quite convinced them, but at least, they stop arguing and follow the teleportation order. Once both young men obey, Daniel teleports to Bastion, grateful most Seekers can always return to the capital if they set up an open contract declaring it their base of operations.

As expected, Daniel appears in the center of the portal room.

Something hard slams into his back.

Rolling forward, Daniel calls a short sword from the Veil. He takes a defensive position and tries to gauge where a new attack will come from. Somebody seizes the two apprentices and hustles them out of the room. Torches lining the room let him see the dozen huntsmen spread throughout the room and the large number of men wearing the yellow and green uniforms of Pirok Guards flanking the Supreme Huntmaster. The man who hit Daniel moves next to Jordan looking smug.

Daniel straightens but keeps his sword angled defensively.

"Lay down your weapon, Daniel," says Jordan. "You're under arrest."

"On what charges?" Daniel demands.

"Dereliction of duty for one thing," Huntmaster Pine says, idly tapping the bo staff against the ground for emphasis.

Daniel shakes his head.

"You would not have gathered a force for that, even if you had the foresight to predict I would return today without finishing the training."

"The other charge is much worse," Pine announces. He stands taller, relishing his news. "You stand accused of conspiring with Saroth agents to kill your Supreme Huntmaster."

Anger and worry grapple inside Daniel. He sweeps his gaze over Jordan to check for wounds.

"What is my motive for wanting to kill you?" Daniel directs the question to his friend before sending his sword back into the Veil.

"You tell us," demands Pine.

"I have no answer because there is none," Daniel says, growing weary of the ridiculous accusation. "And we have more important matters to discuss. What happened to Christa?"

"Lady Christa Lekros is none of your concern," Pine answers, "but perhaps that answers the motive question."

"Do you love her?" asks Jordan.

The question hits Daniel harder than Pine's bo staff. A memory of a similar scene comes to him. Soon after Daniel's triumphant return with young Shadow, Pine and Jordan had questioned him about his relationship with Christa. That had ended when a messenger arrived with news of Marina's trouble.

"She's an old friend," Daniel answers. "I want to help her. If you let me read the room—"

"Out of the question," Pine declares, turning to Jordan. "We should only have untainted Seekers involved in the investigation, Supreme Huntmaster."

"I can see what happened," Daniel finishes, ignoring Pine as usual. He musters as much conviction as possible but doubts still creep in. Reading a room's history isn't the most glamorous of Seeker Gifts, but it has served Daniel well in the past.

"I already know what happened," Jordan answers slowly. "Take him to a holding cell. I'll question him myself tomorrow."

Daniel tenses as two Pirok Guards step forward and reach for his arms. He concentrates on not shoving the left guard, disarming the right one, and teleporting out of the portal room. The left guard gestures, and enchanted ropes bind Daniel's wrists tightly in front of his body.

"At least call Kyle Ricci," Daniel begs. "He's a Destroyer with some power over diseases. He may be able to save her."

"I already know how to save her."

Daniel ponders Jordan's statement as the guards escort him down to the prison level located directly below Deliverance Hall. The Supreme Huntmaster's expression haunts Daniel.

How can he be that certain?

Daniel walks as slowly as possible. Even with enchanted ropes, he could teleport back to the portal room and try to escape, but that would ruin any chance of talking Jordan into letting him see Christa. He also needs to know why Jordan thinks he would attack him. Unfortunately, every path to answers involves spending at least the night in prison.

Chapter 11:
Our Guest

Polani Estate, City of Jorash
Same night as Daniel's arrest (About ten months after Marina's death)
(Vic is a year and a half old; Christa's twins are about seven and a half years old)

"It's late," says Gabriel. "We should wait until Marcus arrives and see what he says. Vic's already asleep."

"You heard the same message I did," Tielle argues. "Daniel stands accused of plotting against the Supreme Huntmaster." A lump of fear burns her throat. "This will never reach a normal court. His life lies in the hands of a council he's defied many times. If he's asking to see her, it's probably bad."

"We don't even know if the request comes from Daniel," says Gabriel. "These are the same people who kept my sister in prison because it suited them."

"They won't do that to him." Tielle hates arguing with her husband, but she also believes Daniel deserves to see his daughter. "Daniel is Arkonai. Moreover, he's a respected member of the Guild. They will have to give him a public trial, even if it is rigged."

"Pardon the second interruption, but this just arrived at the portal," announces a servant. He clutches a black arrow with speckled gray fletching. "A messenger is awaiting a response."

Fighting a feeling of dread, Tielle rushes over to the servant and accepts the black arrow.

"I'm missing something," Gabriel mutters. "Why do you both

look upset?"

"The current Supreme Huntmaster grew up in Aridel," Tielle explains. "They developed a colored arrow system because of the city's unique, tiered structure."

"A courier friend in Outreach explained it to me," says the servant. "Black means danger or threat."

Gabriel moves to Tielle's side as she unfurls the scroll wrapped around the arrow.

Bring Victoria Saveron to Deliverance Hall tonight to visit her father, or she will never see him again.

Tielle tries to read the message again, but it disappears, leaving only blank parchment behind. It doesn't matter. The words still burn against her conscience. She turns to fetch Vic, but Gabriel catches her arm.

"Where are you going?" Gabriel asks. "You can't possibly consider bringing Vic into that kind of danger."

"What choice do we have?" asks Tielle.

"None," says the servant. His voice stays the same, but his demeanor shifts to exude more confidence.

Gabriel takes his wolf form and leaps in front of Tielle, growling.

The false servant merely grins.

"Please don't do anything foolish," he says, cradling a small lightning bolt between his hands. "When my colleague arrives, I can explain the situation better."

Gabriel takes a menacing step forward but stops when the Destroyer casts the lightning bolt into the floor between them.

"I can form these faster than you can move," says the Destroyer. "My master has bid me to spare you if I can, but it's not a binding order. Return to your human form if you want your wife to live."

Tielle's heart lurches.

Gabriel's growl rumbles louder, then changes pitch as he shifts back to human form. He stands with hands forming tight fists.

Tielle steps up beside him and grips his right arm. The move serves the dual purpose of comforting him and steadying her nerves. He's impulsive enough to attack the Destroyer.

The door opens and another servant man appears cradling Katrina. She's sleeping in her puppy form. The thin leather collar encircling her neck sends out subtle waves of dark energy from the line of embedded clear crystals.

"What did you do to her? What is that thing?" Tielle whispers the horrified questions.

"She's only sleeping," says the Destroyer. "The collar will prevent her from changing forms."

"Remove that from her immediately." Gabriel's voice vibrates with disgust and rage.

"It will be removed once your wife retrieves the other child," explains the Destroyer.

"Get her yourself," Gabriel snaps.

"Gabriel!" Tielle pours her fear and surprise into his name.

"The room is warded," the Destroyer explains. "She is the only one capable of entering the child's room at this hour."

"How do you know that?" Tielle demands. Nobody was supposed to know about that plan, not even Gabriel.

"Lady Corabelle told me so I could update the staff," says the Destroyer. "Please stop stalling. Go get the child and return, or we kill both Shapeshifters."

"Tielle, don't!" Gabriel pleads, catching her hand as she pulls away. "We have to protect Vic."

"I have to protect you and Katrina," Tielle whispers. Blinking back tears, she breaks Gabriel's hold and moves toward the door.

The Destroyer gallantly steps aside and swings the door open for her.

"We'll be waiting," he says.

Alternating between silent, incoherent prayers and the mind equivalent of frantic shouts, Tielle races to the room set aside for Vic. Clutching the sides of the crib, Tielle gazes down at the sleeping toddler. Misery nearly overwhelms her, but fear for Gabriel and Katrina gives her strength.

Can I really do this? Can I trade one life for another?

Watching Vic sleep restores some peace to Tielle.

"Pick her up," commands the Destroyer.

Tielle shakes her head, resigned to her fate but refusing to endanger Vic. She instinctively holds her breath and waits for a lightning bolt to end her life.

Vic's crib bursts into flames.

Instinctively, Tielle plucks Vic off the cushion and stumbles back from the crib.

A heavy hand lands on her shoulder.

The flames disappear.

The bedroom vanishes.

They appear in a portal room surrounded by armed men. Half of the men wear bright yellow and green tunics over plain pants. The remaining men have on traditional huntsmen clothes.

The Destroyer releases Tielle's shoulder.

She holds Vic closer, but the baby hardly stirs.

Without a word of greeting, the man flanked by the most guards tosses a pouch to the Destroyer.

The pouch clinks when caught.

Bowing, the Destroyer steps through the portal leading to the Alamon Temple.

"Escort them down to Daniel." The leader has messy light brown hair and features that look like they could be pleasant if he didn't scowl so fiercely. "Let them visit for a while, then prepare a containment suite. I need to speak with Daniel in private."

"Are you certain that's wise?" asks a man standing to the leader's left. "She's a Saroth."

"She's our guest," corrects the leader, keeping his sharp eyes on Tielle. "We requested she deliver the daughter of one of our people, and she has done so. What occurred outside our lands has no bearing on our stance."

"Why are you holding Daniel?" Tielle moves Vic to a new position to ease her aching arms.

The man near the leader stands taller, brown eyes widening and nostrils flaring.

"Watch your tone, Saroth," he says. "You stand before the Supreme Huntmaster of the Arkonai Hunting Guild." He waves to the leader.

Tielle looks at the man in a new light. This must be Jordan Lekros. She knows little about him except that he came by the position in an unusual manner, and he was once Daniel's close friend.

"He's your friend," says Tielle. "That should mean something."

"It does. That's why he's alive." Frustration smolders in the Supreme Huntmaster's eyes.

Tielle suspects that's not nearly the whole truth, but with no more proof than a gut feeling, she follows guards down several flights of stairs and through some long hallways to a prison wing. The long room has been divided into three cells. Daniel occupies the middle one. Tielle quickens her steps as she nears her friend.

Daniel had been sitting on a cot with his head in his hands, but once he spots Tielle, he gets up and stands before the door. He wears a pair of thin metal bracelets that remind her of Vic's bracers. She glances at the toddler's right wrist to confirm the bracers are still in place.

"What are you doing here?" asks Daniel.

"I was forced to bring Vic to you," Tielle answers. The story pours forth in one long stream. "I'm sorry," Tielle finishes.

By this time, one guard opens the cell door, and another instructs Tielle to hold out her right wrist.

Too tired to fight the man, Tielle obeys. A metal bracelet slides into place before a hard shove sends her across the threshold into the cell.

Daniel catches her.

The gems surrounding the bracelet light up as the enchanted metal shrinks to fit her wrist. She eyes the contraption warily, aware that such a security measure once brought great harm to Marina.

"You should sit down," says Daniel. Getting no response, he slowly slips Vic out of Tielle's arms. "Please, sit before you collapse. I'm already feeling guilty they involved you."

"I don't understand any of this," Tielle laments, sinking onto the cot. "Why would your Supreme Huntmaster falsely accuse you of anything?"

Daniel doesn't answer right away. Instead, he spends a quiet moment holding Vic. When she stirs, Daniel paces the cell. It only takes him four small paces to cross the cell's length, but the movement has a calming effect on Tielle.

She hopes someday she'll get to see Gabriel hold their child.

"My friend, Christa, has been poisoned."

Daniel's statement further confuses Tielle.

"I'm not sure why that matters, but I think it's important," Daniel continues. "I returned to see if I could visit my friend and was met by guards and huntsmen. I figured it was a misunderstanding, and I didn't want to kill anybody for following orders."

"The Supreme Huntmaster has men preparing a containment suite so he can question you," says Tielle. "Why would he do that?"

"I'm not sure," Daniel admits. "The prison should have nullifier properties to prevent prisoners from accessing their Gifts. A containment suite has some added layers of protection against using magic, but that doesn't answer why Jordan would bother lying or involving you."

"Could it be about Vic?" Tielle wonders, hoping that's not the case.

"Maybe," Daniel says thoughtfully. "But what could Jordan gain from such a deal?"

"My wife's life," answers the Supreme Huntmaster's voice from outside the cell.

Tielle glances up surprised to find a solitary hooded figure instead of the previous two guards.

"Give the child to the Saroth woman, Daniel," says the Supreme Huntmaster. "I don't want her to get hurt."

Seething, Daniel transfers Vic back into Tielle's arms.

"Keep her bracers on at all times." Pain twists Daniel's features as the security bracelets flare.

"Go to the containment suite and wait for me, or I'll have you dragged there," says the Supreme Huntmaster.

"He won't hold you long," Daniel promises. "Keep my girl safe. I'll try to sort this as quickly as possible."

Tielle tries to respond but cannot find any words. Helpless, she watches Daniel march out of the cell and turn right, moving deeper into the prison.

"Lie down." The Supreme Huntmaster waves a scroll at her. "The sleep scroll's effects will be less painful if there's no room to fall."

Tielle moves further back on the cot and squeezes Vic tightly. The fact that the child's still sleeping tells her it must be an unnatural rest. A wave of bone-deep weariness sweeps over Tielle. She blinks rapidly, fighting the effects. Leaning against the wall, she braces her arms, so Vic won't tumble free when the scroll has its inevitable victory over her senses.

"I'll have my people take you home soon."

The last thing Tielle feels before losing consciousness is Vic's warm, reassuring weight being lifted off her chest.

Chapter 12:
Ransom and Relief

Private Gardens, Supreme Huntmaster's Estate, City of Bastion
Three days after Daniel's arrest (Ten months after Marina's death)
(Vic is a year and a half old; Christa's twins are about seven and a half years old)

Jackson arrives at the appointed hour to find an agitated Supreme Huntmaster waiting for him.

"Give me the antidote," Jordan demands.

"You have not fulfilled our master's requests," says Jackson. "Why should you be rewarded for failure?"

"I did not fail," Jordan declares. "I sent Daniel to the Enchanted Forest as agreed. He returned early because he found out about Christa being poisoned. I have his child, and Daniel has been contained."

Does he speak truth, Master?

To a point. The prison should prevent Daniel from interfering, but the Enchanted Forest would be better. We may yet prevail though. Have him kill Daniel, then I can send another agent by to dispose of the child.

"Kill Daniel and that portion of the bargain will be counted complete," says Jackson.

"He's in my custody. I cannot kill him," Jordan argues.

"Why not? I have heard Arkonai justice can be swift," says Jackson. "Hire men to swear Daniel plotted against you and let your laws deal with him."

"He's too well-liked for me to get a conviction based on testimony alone, and I cannot arrange an assassination on such short notice, even with a secret contract. Perhaps you—"

"I'm not doing your job for you," Jackson says, cutting the Supreme Huntmaster off.

"Then give me another task because this one is impossible."

I do like the idea of him being beholden to us. Perhaps a **new deal is possible. Have our friend prove he controls the child.**

"Show me the child."

Do not touch her. You and Jordan must remain innocent of Victoria's blood.

With a tight nod, Jordan leads the way through several winding paths.

What does it matter if Victoria dies now? The Arkonai leader would work very hard to keep that story from spreading, especially if the death happens in his private gardens.

Very few Conjurers have your ability to move about at will. Suspicion would fall to you. Your mother has already made several inquiries since the Saroth woman's safe return. We cannot yet afford the attention.

Though smaller than the gardens behind the Castaloni estate on the outskirts of Outreach, Jackson admires the variety of plants and the care taken to provide a peaceful setting. Flowering plants that normally would not bloom this time of year or so high on the continent flourish side by side. Marina would have been able to name them, but Jackson never cared enough for plant studies to know more than a few basic flowers. He recognizes lilies, amaryllis, carnations, poppies, and a few more but nowhere near the dozens he passes.

As the path turns out of sight, Jackson slows his steps, suddenly wary of the isolation.

Laughter reaches out and sets him at ease.

Rounding the corner, Jackson steps from the path into a small, artificial clearing. At the center, he finds a boy about seven or eight holding a wooden sword in a guarded position against a fair-haired toddler clutching a wooden dagger. Having no interest in the mock duel, the toddler shrieks and waves the dagger about with abandon. Spotting their audience, the boy drops his wooden sword and sweeps the toddler up into his arms.

"This is my son, Shadow," says Jordan.

The introduction is unnecessary. A black mask covers the bottom half of the boy's face, but his hair and eye colors match the Supreme Huntmaster perfectly.

"And you know Victoria," Jordan adds. "Will you be taking her now?"

The boy doesn't bother bowing. Instead, he holds the child protectively.

Oblivious to the charged atmosphere, Victoria reaches up and touches the boy's face mask.

"Doh!" Victoria cries.

The boy backs up a step and catches the girl's hand before she can grasp the mask.

"Of course not," Jackson replies. Turning around, he starts back the way they had come. He waits another dozen paces before speaking, not wishing the boy to hear their conversation. "The Master will send an agent for the child later tonight. When I get confirmation of the transfer and Daniel's death, I will deliver the antidote. I trust you can clear the way for that to happen."

"I told you. I cannot kill Daniel," says Jordan. "Not here and not under these circumstances. Give me time to fulfill the order, and I will do it."

"Your wife cannot afford such a delay," Jackson points out. "My potions master informed me that his original estimates may have been slightly optimistic. I thought she would have two full weeks, but he tells me it's closer to one. It's been almost three days since Lady Christa accepted the poison. Surely reports have confirmed she's not faring well."

Jackson suddenly finds his back pressed against a tree trunk and a dagger nestled under his chin.

"How about your life, Saroth?" Jordan asks. "Does your master value that?"

A chuckle rolls through Jackson's mind.

Jordan's startled expression says he must hear the same.

I do. I value all my servants, including you.

"I'm not your servant," Jordan mutters. "I will never—"

Before you utter any vows, hear my new terms.

The Supreme Huntmaster doesn't look pleased, but he releases Jackson, tucks the dagger away, and retreats a step.

I will accept delivery of Daniel's child as satisfactory partial payment. In return, I will have my servant cure your wife. Meanwhile, you will turn your thoughts to removing Daniel permanently.

"Why do you wish him dead?" Jordan wonders, "and what will you do to his child?"

You do not need that knowledge, and it is better you do not have it.

"Christa would never forgive me for considering this," Jordan laments.

She will never know. Do we have a deal?

"I'm risking a lot. I want better terms." Jordan's shoulders lift defensively.

Better terms require better service. What can you do for me?

"I am the Supreme Huntmaster." Jordan's chin tips up defiantly. "My word is law to many and heeded by many more. I can direct that power to any cause you wish me to champion."

Intriguing offer. What would you like in return?

"Protection for my wife and son, a position of power, and help with removing my enemies."

The immediacy of Jordan's answer indicates he has given the matter much thought. Jackson's opinion of the man rises.

We will discuss this more later. My servant has an errand to run, and you have an assassination to plan.

Despite being annoyed at the dismissal, Jackson offers the Supreme Huntmaster a brief bow.

"Send the proper messages to remove your guards from Lady Christa's room, and I will deliver the counteragent tonight."

Jackson opens the Veil and slips through to Fort Medron to await new orders. He spends the rest of the afternoon and the first portion of the evening studying incantations for creating Darkland portals. Deep in the Temperance Library archives, Jackson had uncovered several rare tomes containing the forbidden knowledge. He'd bought a similar scroll from a broker working through Lady Sierra's House of Discreet Transactions in Outreach. He suspects that one might be a well-prepared scam, but he cannot afford to miss out on the chance it's genuine.

The portals he has created over the last several months have been improvements upon the first, but they're still far too temporary to be useful in letting his master's armies cross over into Aeris properly. Zombies summoned through scrolls are fragile creatures. Those stepping through a portal can be controlled better because of their stronger connection to the Darklands. According to his latest research, it may be possible to summon certain Darkland beings like Denkari through rituals unrelated to portal creation, but the energy requirements are much the same or even more demanding.

The child is being picked up presently. You should eat something before making your delivery.

Accepting the words as an order, Jackson conjures a vegetable stew and a loaf of fresh bread from his table in the Jorash estate. He consumes the food too quickly to really enjoy it. A strange sensation moves through his stomach at the prospect of facing the beautiful Arkonai woman again. Guilt creeps over him at causing her such distress.

This is war. Uncomfortable things must be done. Besides, tonight, you get to be her hero.

Not wishing to be drawn into a discussion with his master, Jackson travels through the Veil to the lady's room inside the Shadow Oaks estate in the city of Aridel. Realizing he's not alone, Jackson slips his hand into his robes for a dagger.

Wait. It's just the girl. Speak with her.

By this time, the girl has risen from her perch on the bed. The energy orbs placed around the room brighten at her movement. The scene resembles the night the lady took the poison, but this time, the child blocks Jackson's path to the bed and the woman lies unconscious. Having seen the girl's twin only hours before, Jackson compares them. Her brown hair is a little darker than the boy's hair. Whereas the boy seemed timid, the girl brims with barely restrained anger.

"Stay away!" cries the girl. She holds her hands out defensively. "I'm a Destroyer. I'll hit you with lightning if you come too close."

Reassure her you are there to aid her mother and send the girl away. Now is not the time for revelations.

Calling the counteragent to hand, Jackson makes sure the girl can clearly see the glass container of blue liquid.

"I have brought the cure," he announces.

"Did you do this to her?" the girl demands, not budging from her protective position.

Be cautious. She is a Seeker and may know if you lie to her.

"I did," Jackson admits. "I needed your father to do something for me."

The girl's blue eyes widen with fear.

"He has completed his task," says Jackson, ignoring her reaction. "Hence, my presence with the cure for your mother. If you retire to your room, I will administer it, and she should recover by morning."

The fear etched into the girl's features turns to concern and curiosity.

"May I give it to her?" she asks.

I see no problem with this. Let the child feel useful.

"As you wish," Jackson replies, holding out the vial.

The girl covers the space between them with a few furtive steps. Once she secures the counteragent vial, she rushes back to her mother's side. The Arkonai woman barely breathes. A white cloth rests upon her forehead. Sweat has matted her lovely golden hair, but the helpless state enhances her innate beauty.

Gently, the girl angles the woman's face so she can pour in the liquid. At first, she pours too quickly, and some dribbles out of the patient's mouth. From that moment on, the girl slows the administration to an agonizing drop by drop pace.

Though he could safely leave, Jackson watches the cure being delivered.

As the final drops tumble from the vial, the lady opens her eyes. First, she spots her daughter and smiles weakly. Next, she looks past the child to Jackson and tries to sit up.

Gesturing for calm, Jackson moves closer, so she won't have to strain to see him.

"The ransom has been paid. You will live," Jackson announces. Using his Gift, he plucks the empty vial out of the girl's hand.

"What? Who?" The woman's voice fails before she can air more questions.

Lady Christa wishes to know the details of the ransom. You may tell her, but the knowledge will hurt her. The affection she bears for Daniel and Victoria runs deep. She will carry significant guilt if she finds out their lives were the ransom.

"I will not burden you with details," says Jackson, "but rest assured, your part in this is finished. No further threat will fall to you or your household concerning these matters."

Lady Christa nods and reaches for her daughter's hand.

"Leave." The girl's jaw trembles as she fights her emotions.

Suddenly weary, Jackson returns to Fort Medron to rest and think.

"Is Victoria dead yet?" he wonders.

Not yet but soon. I'm hoping Jordan can return Daniel to the Enchanted Forest, but he will not stay there if his daughter is missing. We cannot keep that quiet if somebody alerts the Minder. I have tied him up with Tariku League meetings, but that is a temporary fix. Perhaps it's time for a heart-to-heart with Marcus Polani.

Chapter 13:
Livali

Prison Level below Deliverance Hall, City of Bastion
Same day (About ten months after Marina's death)
(Vic is a year and a half old)

Daniel studies the cracks and pits in the prison cell's stone floor. He has mentally mapped them dozens of times over the past few days. If he concentrates hard enough, the exercise soothes him, allowing him to forget his friend could be dying and his daughter has become a High Council hostage. Occasionally, he can work up the energy to exercise, but mostly, he tries to think through escape plans and weigh the consequences of enacting them.

Once they bring him up to the main council chamber, he should be able to access his Gifts again. However, the ability to escape does not improve his situation. Leaving before being cleared of the ridiculous charges would only prompt the High Council to write a legitimate contract against him. Given Jordan's erratic behavior, Daniel cannot predict the provisions of such a contract. He wants to believe they would insist on a clean capture, but many huntsmen care only about obtaining their quarry, not the morality involved in the hunt.

As before when Daniel let the arrest happen, he refuses to be a reason innocent people get hurt. The conviction solidifies in his heart.

What should I do?

Waiting for the Council to decide his fate goes against his nature. A fair trial would exonerate him, but many previous experiences have taught him that politics could easily control the outcome, regardless of truth. Lord Terrence and Huntmaster Ibish would demand absolute

80

proof before letting Daniel be executed, but Jordan and Pine likely wouldn't have leveled the accusation in the first place unless they had something credible. The resulting scandal would cast a sour light upon the Council either way.

Why do it? There's no win for him.

The sound of footsteps draws Daniel's attention up from the floor cracks before he can attempt answering the question. Spotting Tielle and several others approaching rapidly, he leaps to his feet and moves to the cell's center. The security bracelets tingle, reminding him to remain in the cell. His confusion spikes much higher as he spots the people close on Tielle's heels. Lord Terrence, Huntsman Callen, Lady Ireena, and young Tellen.

Daniel bows to his visitors and greets them by name.

"What brings everybody to the prison level?" His gaze lingers on Tellen.

The boy stands tall and lifts his chin.

"My da's going to save you," the boy announces.

Lady Ireena kneels beside the boy and grips his shoulders, suppressing a grin.

"Hush, love. Let your father and Lady Tielle handle this." A worried look settles on her face as she looks to Callen. She draws Tellen closer, wrapping her arms around the boy.

Callen's stance and expression read both determined and concerned.

Lord Terrence wears a deep frown.

Tielle shifts her weight from foot to foot, likely a habit she picked up from her husband. She appears excited, nervous, and slightly defiant.

"What have you done?" Daniel directs the question to Tielle with his eyes. He doesn't need his Gifts to know the crazy, unvoiced plan originates with her.

"I found a way to set you free!" says Tielle. "The Hunting Guild has an ancient custom called livali. It means—"

"'Life for life,'" Daniel finishes. The custom fell out of practice ages ago. Few people trust each other enough to honor such bargains. Instead of an item or sum of money, Livali allows another person to stand in for a prisoner. If the prisoner fails to return by the appointed time, their fate falls to the substitute.

"Exactly," Tielle confirms. "Huntsman Callen has agreed to take your place until the trial. It's set for the day after tomorrow."

Daniel shakes his head wearily, looking at the grim faces arrayed before him.

"It's not necessary," he says. "I can await the—"

"It is necessary," Callen counters.

"Vic's gone." Tielle tries to deliver the words gently, but it's impossible.

"Gone?" Daniel mumbles the word like he has never heard it before. He steps back, then plants his feet and glares at everybody. "What do you mean she's gone? Jordan said she would be at his estate in this city."

"She was until a few hours ago," says Lord Terrence. "Somebody picked her up claiming to be acting upon orders from Lady Corabelle."

Daniel stalks to the far corner of his cell.

"That makes no sense!" Daniel cries. "Jordan would never recognize Lady Corabelle's authority. She's Saroth. She doesn't exist to him."

"He's claiming the move was made to foster trust between Arkonai and Saroth," explains Lord Terrence. "I didn't believe him, so I contacted Marcus Polani. He sent Lady Tielle. She has been researching our customs since her return home after your arrest. She explained the plan to me, and I brought it to Callen and his family. It was their decision to come."

"Why would you let them?" Daniel asks, simultaneously exasperated and grateful.

"You're a Seeker. You're the only one who can save your daughter," says Lady Ireena, "and you're a good man. You'll return for their sakes." She sounds nervous.

The terror hovering beneath Lady Ireena's cool expression suddenly makes sense.

They brought Tellen to stand in for Vic.

"My daughter was never in custody," Daniel points out.

"She was under the Supreme Huntmaster's protection until somebody came to claim her," says Callen. "To save face, he has to pretend it's a sanctioned outing. The only way he gets to do that is to let this bargain stand."

Turning to his father, Callen holds out his wrists. Lord Terrence quickly slips two security bracelets into place and activates the gems. They blink several times, giving Callen time to step into the cell with Daniel. The process repeats with Tellen and Lady Ireena, but they fit the security bracelets to the child's ankles instead of his wrists.

"You don't have to stay, Ireena," says Callen. "You should visit

Lady Christa."

"There will be time for that later," says Lady Ireena, sitting on the cot with Tellen. Her tone ends further arguments about leaving her son.

The boy sits down to examine the fancy pieces of metal on his ankles.

"These are heavy," says Tellen. "Why do I have to wear them?"

Lady Ireena leans over and answers him quietly, ending the speech with a kiss on his hair.

"Why are you doing this?" Daniel demands, struggling to understand his friends. "You know I will try to return, but a hundred things could go wrong."

"We wouldn't be here if Marina didn't willingly step into harm's way for us," says Callen. He looks at his wife and son. "If a few hours in this cell will let you find Vic, so be it."

He leaves unsaid the consequences of Daniel never returning or coming back without his daughter.

"I will not forget your courage or your kindness," Daniel declares with a solemn bow.

Lord Terrence deactivates and removes the security bracelets before holding a scroll out to Daniel.

"Sign this," he orders. "It's a contract for your daughter. Hopefully, it will let you use more of your Gifts in the search. The young lady and I will try to summon the rest of the Council. These matters should be completed tonight."

Daniel accepts the enchanted scroll, confirms Lord Terrence's claim about it being a contract for Vic, and signs it. He's surprised to find the contract written on Tielle's behalf until he remembers she and Gabriel are Vic's house sponsors.

"Find Vic," says Tielle, hugging Daniel as he steps out of the cell. "They couldn't have taken her far."

"I will," Daniel promises.

"Marcus said he'll help, but he doesn't know this city." Tielle's words tumble out swiftly. "He'll let you know if he senses her elsewhere. Portals are being watched by huntsmen. Marcus thinks the person or persons who took Vic will try to leave by one of the gates sometime tonight."

Daniel nods then sprints for the exit.

The guards stand straighter as he passes, but they do not try to stop him.

Upon reaching the main level, Daniel stops and spreads his senses outward, trying to get a hint of his daughter's whereabouts. His impatience and urgency impede the effort. Not liking the sense of being watched, he leaves Deliverance Hall by the main entrance and jogs down to the middle of the long flight of stairs leading up to the building.

After several calming breaths, Daniel brings his hands to his chest and closes his eyes to facilitate concentration. Searching for one soul within a city of thousands requires more effort than weeding through lifeforms in a forest since creatures feel different than people.

Daniel casts his Gift sense out until he feels the city limits, rotates his body right, and repeats the process until he has turned a full circle. The first sweep reveals nothing. He tries the same process in reverse, turning left this time. Next, he teleports to the roof of Deliverance Hall, landing on the glass skylight above the main meeting chamber. Wind buffets him. Daniel lets the cold sting of it revive his spirits before returning to the work.

Help me find her.

Daniel's not sure who the simple prayer is aimed at, but Marcus answers him.

She's somewhere east of your current location. I'm sorry I can't narrow it down more. I'm still mapping the city.

East helps.

Daniel orients himself and searches more carefully, trying to distinguish the adult and child presences. It's not a perfect system, but most children have presences that fluctuate like a flickering candle while many adults stay at one level of brightness. The distinction lets him dismiss many presences from consideration.

Since Marcus's clue lets him eliminate half the city of Bastion, Daniel moves his awareness from left to right in ever-expanding semi-circles. The search leads him to Vic's familiar sense just as Marcus finds her too.

Vic's safe, but you're not going to believe who she's with.

Marcus provides a mental beacon for Daniel to follow.

Drawing a short sword from the Veil, Daniel teleports to the location and arrives in a nearly empty Gathering Hall.

A cloaked and hooded figure sits on a stool holding Vic. The hood slips off when the woman raises her head.

Daniel's mind goes blank as he stares at Lady Corabelle, sword hand dropping to his side.

Marina's mother looks older and sadder than she had during

their last meeting a week ago.

"We haven't much time, Daniel," says Lady Corabelle. She drops her gaze back to Vic's sleeping form. "You must return to your friends with your daughter soon, but once things are settled with the High Council, you should disappear."

"Is that a threat?" Daniel asks, tightening his grip on the sword.

"Not from me, but a threat exists," says Lady Corabelle, meeting his eyes. Her voice hardens as she continues, "Do you know how I came by Victoria this evening?"

"Tell me," Daniel says curtly. He sends the sword into the Veil.

"One of my people told me of a contract placed on her life," says Lady Corabelle. "The existence of such did not surprise me. There are several others, but the location and timing did. I do not like that your Supreme Huntmaster has involved himself in this."

"On that we agree," Daniel says darkly. "I'll deal with him."

"That would only cause more trouble." Climbing down from the stool, Lady Corabelle passes Vic over to Daniel. "Keep her away from Caramore and Bastion until we can sort through the current threats."

"Is this about the inheritance?" asks Daniel. He changes Vic's position so her head rests upon his right shoulder.

"Only in the sense that I want Victoria to live long enough to claim it," answers Lady Corabelle.

"Should I have her forfeit the rights to the holdings?" Daniel inquires, rubbing Vic's back as he considers the request. He hates the idea of his daughter facing unknown dangers from multiple sides. Plus, his treatment the last few days has strained his last few strands of loyalty for the Arkonai Hunting Guild.

"For better or worse, we are far past that point," says Lady Corabelle. "You don't have to quit the Guild, but you should avoid cities for a few years." With a snap, she sends the stool away. "I will let you know when the danger diminishes to a point I'm comfortable the opportunists have moved on."

"I will consider your advice, Lady Corabelle." Closing his eyes, Daniel teleports back to Deliverance Hall.

Chapter 14:
New Trouble

Marina's Final Resting Place, Karnok Mountains
Two years and four months after Marina's death
(Vic is three years old)

Corabelle sets the Teleportation scroll for the edge of the clearing near Marina's final resting place. Despite the tremendous amount of work involved in creating such scrolls, she had personally crafted this one, considering the many hours of complicated spell work a labor of love. If she had advanced along in the Conjuring arts as much as her son, Jackson, she could have moved through the Veil to her desired location. But studies that intense have a way of becoming completely consuming. Antonio had come along at a time in her life when she had barely begun seriously developing her Gifts.

Letting her feet travel the well-worn path from the clearing's edge to the grave, Corabelle wonders what life would look like if she had ignored the handsome, highborn man's advances. She might still be working for the Castaloni holdings, creating Teleportation and Transportation scrolls for a living. It's respectable work, but certainly not something that would carry her to the Tariku League's meeting chambers.

Several amaryllis plants grow around the grave. Corabelle pauses her approach to admire them. The beautiful flowers feature proud red edges with soft white centers.

They suit her well.

A plain headstone sits between the amaryllis plants. Kneeling, Corabelle places her right hand on the flat stone and closes her eyes. An image of Marina forms inside her mind. Though warned that would happen, the depth and clarity of the mental picture makes her draw a sharp breath.

Marcus Polani had worked with Navina Christol and a few other Minders to pull several images of Marina from their collective memories and weave them into an enchantment placed upon the headstone. He didn't possess the right Gifts to accomplish the task alone, but he proposed the idea of enchanting the stone so Victoria would have a piece of her mother to cherish.

Tears drip down Corabelle's face as she slowly cycles through the memories a second time. The first shows a red-faced, frantic Marina carrying a small child. The next has her sitting on a cot in a plain cell, laughing at something. The third consists of a few seconds of her wedding to Daniel. The fourth shows her binding a patient's wounded arm. The fifth stars Marina and a newborn baby. Corabelle recalls the scene of Raelyn tucking Victoria into Marina's arms for the first time. The last shows only Marina's head and shoulders. The expression captured perfectly defined her: fierce, loving, stubborn, kind, patient, and good to a fault.

Corabelle's heart aches anew for both of her slain daughters, the one she bore and the one she adopted.

Marina and Gabriella.

The official investigations into their murders went nowhere. The dead servant found near Gabriella certainly bore some guilt, but Corabelle knew that wasn't the whole tale. Daniel had been cleared of wrongdoing. The mysterious spirit tormenting him certainly played a large part in Marina's death, but the Dark Man had to have help. No spirit could access the natural world long enough to carry out the murder.

I wish you could both see your daughters growing up so quickly.

Though still less than six years old, Katrina Polani had been spontaneously manifesting her Shapeshifter Gift for several years. According to Marcus, Arabeth Talini had offered to begin privately training her soon. Corabelle doesn't know her personally, but the lady's solid reputation precedes her. She used to work for the Academy of Arts and Sciences in Dominance, but in recent years, she's traveled widely to work with the most promising young Shapeshifters. Once upon a time, Corabelle and Antonio had considered hiring her to train Gabriel, but ultimately, they had decided he would benefit from a more traditional form of schooling.

"Victoria should be showing signs of her Gifts soon," says Corabelle, finally lifting her fingers off the headstone.

The images fade away, but they leave her with a lingering feeling of peace.

"No matter which magic school her Gifts come from, Daniel and I will make sure she receives proper training, and Daria Toscano will fill in any educational gaps."

The promise reminds Corabelle of her main purpose in making this trip, introducing Daria to Victoria and Daniel. Throughout the months since Daniel heeded her advice to retreat someplace safe, Tielle had stayed with Victoria whenever Daniel needed to travel. That arrangement would no longer be possible.

"Tielle's going to have a child soon," says Corabelle. "Gabriel's beside himself. He couldn't even get the announcement out. He kept cycling forms until Tielle delivered the news. I've never seen them so happy. Tielle's good for your brother. Perhaps your children can be friends one day."

Her thoughts turn to the possible dangers Victoria may have to face. Under Gabriel's direction, the holdings have fully recovered from the setbacks experienced in the weeks after Marina's murder. They have even begun expanding again, albeit slower than previous years. Thriving businesses mean more opportunists waiting to sweep in and seize control. Oddly, Jackson has not renewed his bid to control the holdings.

"Gabriel will see that Victoria has an inheritance to receive." Climbing to her feet, Corabelle smiles down at the headstone. "But I suspect you'd be more interested in Victoria herself, as am I. In truth, I have not seen her in many months. There's too much to do to ensure threats never reach her, but I will cherish the few moments I get with her today."

With little more to say, Corabelle retraces her steps to the clearing's edge and follows the trail through the woods to Daniel's cabin. It has changed since she last saw it. He built an additional bedroom for Victoria and fenced in a section behind the cabin for her to play in.

Excited screams fill the air.

Instead of going to the front door, Corabelle circles the cabin and finds an odd sight.

So, that's what he needed those for.

A few months back, Daniel had requested several dozen cushions. Corabelle would have made the trip and conjured them for him, but an urgent meeting involving Tariku League business had prompted her to send Tielle in her stead. Corabelle had forgotten the request entirely, but now she sees their purpose. Cushions of various size and color line the entire enclosure.

"Watch me!" shouts Victoria. She races from one end to the other, hurling her body into one cushion after another. A haphazard stack of cushions forms a tower off to the left side. In between ramming into the wall cushions, Victoria climbs the stack and leaps onto yet more cushions.

"I see you," Daniel assures the girl.

He and Daria watch from the safe space near the cabin's back door.

I must have taken longer with Marina than I thought.

Reaching the fence, Corabelle leans on the railing.

Daniel and Daria join her.

"I see you have already met," says Corabelle. "I'm sorry to have missed the introductions."

Before either can reassure her, a pure white light bursts from the center of the yard.

"Look out!" Daria cries.

The huntsman and the Destroyer snap into action the same instant a sense of danger strikes Corabelle.

Whirling, she conjures a thick slab of wood and braces it with her hands as an arrow pierces the board near her head. The sight of the arrowhead appearing near her right eye fills her with fear, but her first instinct is to protect her granddaughter. Turning again, she spots Victoria standing in the center. The silver bracelets have morphed into beautiful bracers, which cover the girl's tiny forearms and shine with brilliant white light.

A figure rises on the enclosure's far side, aiming a crossbow at Victoria. As the bolt flies forward, Corabelle reaches for the nearest dozen cushions with her Conjuring Gift and moves them in the way of the bolt. In between the last two cushions, she adds another wooden board.

A satisfying clunking sound rings out.

Having vaulted the fence, Daniel appears at Corabelle's side.

Another arrow comes toward her, but Daniel knocks it aside with his sword.

Daria moves to grab Victoria.

More arrows and bolts zip through the air.

Corabelle conjures more wooden slabs to shield the huddled

pair, but she's aware it might be the last defense she can offer them.

A skeletal figure starts to climb the fence on the far side.

Horror grips Corabelle. She has heard whispers of undead being spotted near remote villages, but she hasn't given them much thought.

Who would raise such creatures?

The Saroth tradition of burning the dead came about during the last Great War to deprive the necromancers of bodies to reanimate. Corabelle can fully appreciate the appeal of that now.

As the undead creature swings its leg over the fence, Daria hurls a lightning bolt into its chest.

The creature bursts into black dust.

Two more zombies reach the fence.

Daniel sends an arrow through each skull, causing the zombies to crumble into dust.

One appears next to Daniel, swinging a sword at his head.

He parries the blow.

Daria sends a weakened lightning bolt into the creature, knocking it back long enough for Daniel to remove its head with his sword.

Leaning heavily on the fence, Corabelle can only watch as another undead figure climbs the fence. Daria conjures another lightning bolt and holds it like a sword.

A beam of light knocks the undead man off his perch. His rage-filled scream ends abruptly as the light consumes him.

Nobody moves.

They wait three full seconds for the attack to resume.

When nothing happens, Daria lets the lightning bolt dissipate.

Daniel, Daria, and Corabelle silently regard each other, questioning whether they each saw the same thing.

"The last blast came from Vic," says Daniel.

They turn to her in awe, only to find her sleeping. Daria scoops her up and carries her over to them for inspection. The bracers once more resemble plain silver bracelets. Other than Vic being sound asleep, there's nothing out of the ordinary.

"Where did those … things come from?" Daria wonders. "Will they return?"

"I don't know," Daniel admits. "Let me check something."

Closing his eyes, Daniel turns in a slow circle and starts into a second circle. Upon reaching a position with his back turned to Corabelle, Daniel jogs into the woods. He returns shortly with a scroll husk. Normally, a scroll can be cleared of the remnants of the current spell and imbued with a new one. However, it's possible to place a secondary spell to erase traces of the first, leaving behind only an empty, burnt out piece of parchment known as a husk.

"They must have been bound to this," says Daniel, waving the scroll remains.

"Was the attack deliberate or accidental?" Daria wonders. "Somebody delving that deep into dark magic might come out here to experiment in peace. The wards surrounding this place are decent. I missed the turn from the path the first time."

Corabelle watches Victoria with a sinking feeling.

"I must report to the Tariku League," she announces, turning to Daniel. "You should ask Marcus about increased security measures."

"I don't want guards," says Daniel.

"He can probably suggest something that doesn't involve additional people," says Daria, "but I can stay until the measures are implemented, if Lady Corabelle agrees." She turns an expectant gaze to Corabelle.

"It's a good idea." Corabelle speaks quickly so Daniel doesn't have time to protest. "Let me conjure a meal for us, then I will take my leave to report to the council."

Daniel climbs the fence.

Corabelle uses the gate built into the back, nudging two cushions aside to gain entry.

They wake Victoria and share a meal of chicken, rice, and beans with blueberries and whipped cream for dessert.

Another half-hour slips away before Corabelle can force herself to stop watching her granddaughter play among the cushions. Dreading the pain of parting, she calls Victoria over, pulls her into a hug, and kisses her cheek.

"Gamma go?" asks Victoria.

"That's right," Corabelle says, forcing a smile as she pulls back, "but first, I have a gift for you."

"No go!" Victoria shouts. Tears pool in her blue eyes.

Corabelle considers conjuring the little red dress here but doesn't want it to get dirty. She pictures Victoria wearing the dress, matching flower hairpiece, and pearl earrings as she conjures them to appear on the couch inside the cabin.

"I have to," she says, placing a hand on the girl's left cheek.

"Why go?" asks Victoria.

"To protect you," Corabelle replies. "Stay with your father. Your gift will be waiting in the cabin."

Daniel pulls Victoria back, so she won't accidentally get swept along during the teleportation.

Corabelle activates the Teleportation scroll before further explanation is necessary.

And to find out who's behind this new trouble.

Chapter 15:
Alec

**Sitting Room Next to Tielle's Private Chambers, Castaloni
Estate, City of Outreach
Two years and ten months after Marina's death
(Vic is three and a half years old)**

What is taking so long?

A warm, buzzing sense of amusement sweeps through Jackson.

**Babies do not arrive instantly. There's quite a bit of work
involved on the mother's part, even with the aid of herbs to dull the
pain.**

*Why can't Mother—or somebody—just conjure the baby from inside to
outside?*

**It's been tried before, but the risks of the magic going awry
are too high. Few wish to needlessly endanger mother or child.
Same reason Healers only apply their Gifts in situations of extreme
peril for the mother. Most accidents involving magic have
irreversible results.**

A bone-chilling scream comes from the next room.

Jackson flinches, but he's gratified to see his brother react
similarly. He's tempted to conjure a sound nullifying scroll and place it
around the entire room, but at this point, a sudden cessation of noise
might snap something in Gabriel.

Taking squirrel form, Gabriel makes seven swift circuits of the
room, then crosses it three times in random zigzag patterns.

Jackson ignores him. He prefers squirrel form over the other
options. In normal human form, Gabriel looks miserable and paces a

very small section of the room. As a beetle, he makes an awful buzzing noise, and as a wolf, he's a danger to himself and the furniture.

Never thought I'd see the day I prefer him as a squirrel.

Typically, Jackson finds the endless energy of the form irksome, but at least the rodent version can occasionally be distracted by nuts. Jackson notices several nut stashes hidden throughout the room, likely placed there by their mother for just this purpose. Conjuring one of the nuts to hand, Jackson tosses it to Gabriel who deftly catches the treat and gnaws at it.

Everything's fine until the next scream from Tielle prompts another shapeshifting cycle from Gabriel. This one ends as a beetle.

Jackson watches his brother fly aimlessly around the room at top speed until the temptation to conjure him into a jar becomes too appealing. Walking to one of the large windows, Jackson pretends to study the expansive gardens below.

How much longer will this take?

It has only been about ten hours. This could potentially take the rest of the evening.

Can you help her?

No. As previously discussed, magic interference can lead to dire consequences. Do you wish to endanger your heir?

Jackson drops the point without answering the rhetorical question and silently curses Gabriel for calling him so early. The advanced studies of the Conjuring arts have made it physically impossible for Jackson to father a child the traditional way. Thus, he must gain an heir through his brother.

The thought of Gabriel makes Jackson turn around. On first glance, he cannot find him in the room, but a few steps change Jackson's perspective enough to spot his brother in wolf form, sitting in front of the door.

A pitiful whine comes from the wolf.

Jackson retreats to the window again.

How long should I leave the child with them?

Several years at least. You do not have the means, will, or patience to be dealing with a baby. Besides, consider your poor mother. Your sister hasn't been dead three years yet. Corabelle deserves another year or two of relative peace before we arrange the next tragedy in her life.

Keep Mother busy enough with her Tariku League duties, and she'll be fine. And I could hire somebody for the child's needs.

Jackson thinks through details that would make the situation feasible. He would need a wet nurse to feed the child. Somebody would need to watch over, clothe, change, and bathe the child regularly as well. His thoughts run circles, checking and double-checking things involved in an infant's survival.

Three women working in shifts ought to suffice. I could convert some rooms in Fort Medron if desperate, but I'm sure Mother would let her only pure grandchild stay in any one of the estates.

You could afford a hundred staff, but the expense is unnecessary. I guarantee nobody will be more dedicated to the child's safety and happiness than Tielle and Gabriel. Moreover, we must plan their eventual demise with care to avoid suspicion. It must be a tragic accident and cannot end without an explanation like Marina's death. The house council would never stand for it.

Seeing the truth in his master's words does not make them easier to bear. Jackson longs to be free of the plotting and planning. The promise of a crown has very little substance to it because there's not even a unified kingdom to conquer. As a naïve young man contemplating this path, he'd known it would take many years for the Master's grand plan to unfold, but he finds it vexing to have so little to show for more than a decade's worth of hard work.

My plans are proceeding well enough. Your powers have progressed nicely. When I found you, you were a mediocre, frustrated Conjurer whose master refused to properly train. I have made you powerful, and you will not waste that potential on a rash scheme.

Yes, Master. You are right, of course. What kind of accident would you like me to arrange?

Gabriel and Tielle travel regularly as part of keeping the holdings viable. They may limit their travels for the next few months to celebrate their new status as parents, but they will eventually return to old patterns. I'm sure we can somehow send them into a dangerous situation or stir up the right enemy to kill them for us.

We must protect—

Another chilling scream from the next room cuts off the thought.

Gabriel adds a sympathetic howl.

Pity strikes Jackson in the chest. He doesn't like witnessing his brother's distress. Anger and contempt wash through him right after the pity.

I shouldn't feel this way! He's nothing to me!

The agitation causes Jackson to take several steps across the large, ornate rug dominating the room's center. Fortunately, he has a good excuse.

You love him. This is natural for siblings. Do not fight it. Embrace the inevitable loss as a worthy sacrifice, but in the moment, comfort him as you did when he was a child.

Back then, a conjured stuffed animal and simple reassurance solved most problems. The idea reminds Jackson of the two gifts prepared for the child to come. For a girl, he has a jewelry box filled with cinnamon, coriander, and a few other spices with symbolic well-wishes. If the child is a boy, Jackson will present him with an enchanted blanket meant to promote peaceful dreams.

He stops walking.

Is it a boy or a girl?

I'm not telling you because that would burden you with knowledge you should not have. You would then have to carry the secret until the birthing process completes to avoid explaining your connection to me. Speak with your brother about it. Perhaps the distraction will be good for him.

Gabriel's still by the door as a wolf, whining softly.

"Have you chosen names yet?" asks Jackson, finding no way to ease into a conversation.

The wolf nods.

"Tell me about them," Jackson says, working hard for a pleasant tone. "What will you call the child if it's a girl?"

Reluctantly, Gabriel takes his human form and stares longingly at the door before answering.

"Adelina Marina."

The nod to their dead sister surprises Jackson more than it should. Gabriel practically worshiped her.

You're jealous.

Swallowing his annoyance, Jackson mutters appropriate assurances it's a perfect name before prompting his brother to reveal what he'll call a boy. He braces but it doesn't help.

"Alec Marino," says Gabriel. "Tielle chose the first names based on their meanings. Adelina means 'noble' and Alec has something to do with being a protector. I chose the middle names to honor Marina."

Jackson absently repeats his approval of the choice before letting silence envelop the room.

Gabriel collapses onto an armchair, looking disheveled.

Can I change the name once the child becomes my heir?

Not without incurring the house council's wrath. Nobody pays attention to middle names anyway. Many people don't even have one. Who would know or care of the link to your sister?

I would. So would Tielle and Gabriel. I'm sure they're dying to fill the child's mind with stories of Marina's many selfless acts.

An angry flush climbs up his neck. Jackson glares at the floor and concentrates on breathing to calm down. He finds it unfair that Marina should haunt him years after her death. If she had let their original plan stand, she would be alive and not need to be honored in such a way.

I know we must wait, but I do not like leaving my heir under their influence longer than necessary. Tielle doesn't even like me.

You did threaten her.

That was years ago. Gabriel has forgiven me. Why can't she?

You made peace with him, not her, but don't worry. Your invaluable service to the holdings these past few years has restored your brother's trust in you.

Jackson indulges in a moment of self-satisfaction. It's gratifying to know the many hours spent laboring over the creation of Transportation or Teleportation scrolls have purchased something he can exploit later. He doesn't even want to think of how many days of his life have been spent making or checking Teleportation scrolls to keep up with the demand. Each one's unique. It's not a matter of copying the same incantation to a scroll. A highly skilled Conjurer needs to use their Gifts to bind the spell to the parchment, leaving enough leeway for the customer to dictate a precise location.

Over the next few hours, Tielle's cries become more frequent and urgent. The Dark Man assures Jackson this means the ordeal will end soon.

Finally, a different cry splits the thick tension in the room.

Gabriel becomes a beetle and zips across the room a few times.

Jackson's heart beats against his chest. Relief and weariness make his legs ache, even as strange emotions make him want to leap up and run. Gabriel's intense need to move seems less crazy during the endless wait for their mother to fetch them. Jackson's so lost in the waiting he doesn't see or hear the door open.

"You may enter." Mother's announcement barely completes before Gabriel darts past her into Tielle's room.

Figuring Gabriel needs a moment with his wife and newborn, Jackson rises slowly, taking the time to observe his mother. She appears weary but content. Liberal silver streaks cut through her black hair. He's never noticed that before. A faint smile forms as she leans on the doorframe and watches the scene inside the room.

Gabriel stands on the bed's right side. Several servant women stand on the opposite side, observing the happy meeting and offering congratulations before filing out with several large bundles of sheets and towels.

The sight reminds Jackson of the epic struggle recently waged to bring new life into the world. His eyes lock on the tiny figure resting on Tielle's chest.

Strange little noises come from the tightly wrapped bundle.

"Gabriel, I'd like you to meet your son, Alec Marino Castaloni." Fresh tears travel the tracks already established on Tielle's face, but her smile is bright and genuine. She hands the infant over to Gabriel.

Alec.

The name echoes rapidly, punctuated by swift heartbeats. Jackson conjures his gift for the boy, but his mother's hand lands on his right shoulder, silently instructing him to wait.

Gabriel deserves the moment. Subtle facial movements describe the awe, shock, and wonder moving rapidly through him.

Similar emotions run through Jackson, but he buries the feelings. He can't stop staring at the baby nestled in Gabriel's arms. Without having seen the boy's face, Jackson loves him fiercely and completely.

Chapter 16:
Summons

Sunroom, Castaloni Estate, City of Jorash
One week later (Two years and ten months after Marina's death)
(Vic is still three and a half years old)

The tight grip around Daniel's neck warns him the coming parting might hold more drama. Getting Vic dressed turned into a battle when the shoes he picked for her weren't the boots she wanted to wear. They managed to weather the teleportation to Bastion without incident because he held her the whole time, but when he put her down to speak with the guard near the traveler's portal to Outreach, she'd thrown a fit. When they got through the portal, she'd thrown a fit. When he picked her up to walk to the Castaloni estate, she'd quieted down instantly, telling him the previous three fits were probably choices.

What will I do when she outgrows the ability to teleport with me?

He didn't relish the thought of the long treks to the nearest village for supplies. Daniel might be able to make it in a day, but travel with a small child would turn it into a two-or-three-day trip.

When she's older camping will be fun.

He clings to the future hope even as he tries to reason with his daughter.

"Look, Vic, we get to meet your cousin, Alec, today," says Daniel.

"No!" Vic bellows directly into his ear.

A baby starts crying, making Daniel feel guilty.

"We can also see Tielle," he continues. "You love Tielle, remember?"

99

Stepping into the sunroom, Daniel nods to Tielle and Ireena. The latter smiles knowingly and whispers something to her son, Tellen.

The boy marches over.

"Will you play with me?" Tellen asks. "Mum says Lady Tielle will conjure sweets for us if we're good. We can play tag, or I can show you a sword trick I learned in Discovery class this week."

"No sword tricks!" calls Ireena. "She's too young for them. Let's show Vic the fountain we explored this morning."

"No!" Vic shouts again. Nevertheless, she turns to survey the room.

Daniel draws hope from the slight decline in conviction in her tone. He mouths thanks to Ireena, which she acknowledges with a nod.

"We can visit again with Master Alec later," says Ireena.

"But he's boring," says Tellen. "All he does is cry."

Tielle laughs and tries to soothe her son.

"He has a point," she notes.

"That is no excuse for poor manners." Ireena fixes Tellen with a stern look. "Not so long ago, you too were once that 'boring,' young man. Give him time to grow."

"Like an hour?" Tellen wonders, completely serious.

"Like a few years," says Ireena, "but come, let us leave the others to visit in peace. You can teach Vic how to count coins in some of the fountains."

Tellen brightens.

"Can I collect them?" he asks.

"Maybe, but we'll have to put them back," says Ireena.

"Come on, Vic," calls Tellen. "We get to play in the fountain!"

Ireena sighs.

"That is not what I said."

"It'll be fine," Tielle assures her. "I'm sure we can find some spare clothes if they need them. You can even let them add some coins if you wish." With a wave, she conjures a handful of coins and has them hover near Ireena.

The lure of shiny things coaxes Vic down from Daniel's arms. She dashes outside after Ireena and Tellen with barely a backward glance.

"I'm sorry for springing this on you," says Daniel. "I could take her with me, but she cannot come into the closed session." He doesn't elaborate but knows his dark expression explains his feelings more thoroughly than words anyway.

"Nonsense," Tielle declares. "I'm delighted to get to see Vic again. I wanted to visit several times, but Gabriel and Lady Corabelle fussed about rising tensions and the dangers of travel. It was easier to heed them than argue." She lifts the baby in her arms. "Then this one appeared, and I've been a little busy. Would you like to hold him?"

"I must go soon, but yes, of course," answers Daniel, crossing the room to where Tielle sits on one of two fancy couches.

She expertly passes him the infant.

The boy opens sleepy eyes long enough to peek at Daniel before settling down to resume his nap. The delicate heft of the baby stirs up memories of holding Vic when she was this new. Daniel cradles Alec low so he can get a clearer view of the infant's tiny features. The boy has worked one hand out of the wrap and tucked a fist near his chin.

"You can leave Vic here as long as you like," Tielle comments, after a short stretch of silence. "I have plenty of help, and I'm sure Tellen will keep her entertained. I can't blame you for not wanting her near the High Council, and I'm a little surprised you're even answering the summons after the way they treated you."

The statement carries Daniel back to the last time he stepped into the High Council's main meeting chamber in Deliverance Hall. That meeting had been baffling. Jordan had dropped the charges of dereliction of duty and conspiring to kill him, offered a perfunctory apology, and released those held under the terms of livali.

No explanation. No investigation. Nothing.

"Did they ever explain how you came under suspicion?" asks Tielle. "Was the threat to the Supreme Huntmaster real?"

Daniel shakes his head to the first question and shrugs to the second.

"The timing of Christa being poisoned fits too well to be a coincidence," says Daniel. "Your sister confirmed that much. She denies knowing more or having an official assignment from either Marcus or Lady Corabelle, but I don't believe her on either point."

After one more peaceful moment enjoying the baby, Daniel returns Alec to Tielle.

"For a spy, Daria's a terrible liar if it's important, so you can probably assume she didn't learn much you need to know," says Tielle.

Daniel's surprised at his friend's candor. He figured a lifetime growing up in and around house intrigue would make her more cautious.

"My sister was working for Marcus at the Academy before Lady Corabelle hired her to watch over Vic in my place." Tielle draws her son closer. "I worry for Daria, but she enjoys safeguarding Vic. And she's a far better protector for her than I could ever be. Have there been any new incidents I should know about?"

"Thankfully, no," says Daniel, knowing she means the zombie attack from a few months back. "And you would most certainly know. I think another incident like that would make Lady Corabelle lock Vic in a vault for the next thirteen years."

"I can see that happening," says Tielle. "Promise you'll come back. Vic needs you."

Daniel does so, then takes his leave before Vic can return and make the parting more painful. He hates having to leave her behind, but his last encounter with the High Council destroyed all remaining trust in them.

Why don't you quit?

He hopes it doesn't come to that because he likes keeping his options open, despite not accepting any Guild contracts since the arrest. As soon as he's out of the warded house, Daniel teleports directly to Bastion.

Only one young huntsman meets him, but instead of leading to the main Council chamber, he guides Daniel down several halls to a much smaller room. Daniel had heard the rumors of Jordan's growing paranoia but not given the claim much credence until now.

They enter a room filled with people. It's arranged like a theater with the Council members arrayed in a semi-circle along the back wall with two sections of spectators in front of them. Daniel recognizes Huntsman Callen, Lady Callista, and a few others as his escort leads him down to the space between the Council and spectators.

He sends the Council a questioning look. Jordan, Huntmaster Emanuel Ibish, Lord Terrence, Lord Frederick Marsh, and Lord Eric Dillworth are the faces he expects to see. The new faces are Huntmaster Mason Pine of Bastion and Huntmaster Gannon of Urdik.

"These huntsmen and ladies are those who expressed an interest in Council affairs," explains Huntmaster Emanuel Ibish. "They were invited to this closed session to observe, so they can experience how the Council addresses your case and others like it."

"You have the right to have them dismissed if you want this discussion to be private," adds Lord Terrence. "Do you consent to their presence?"

Despite a sense of unease, Daniel agrees to let the audience stay. He likes having Callen present.

"I'm not even sure why I was summoned," says Daniel.

"It should be obvious," comments Huntmaster Pine. "You haven't taken a significant Guild contract in over a year. Therefore, you're behind in your dues."

"I can pay them if that's the only issue." Daniel raises a hand to open the Veil and collect the necessary dues, but Jordan stops him.

"It's not the only issue," says Jordan.

"We know you have the money." Pine doesn't bother hiding his bitterness.

Daniel tries to remember when Pine started showing such blatant animosity. The interactions between them had always been minimal until the man became his direct superior during Daniel's teaching days. He had entered the Guild several years before Daniel and barely glanced his direction.

Until my marriage.

"The bigger issue to some is your non-Guild work."

Lord Terrence's explanation stops Daniel from musing about Pine's Resolute philosophies.

"They're not contracts, so it's not against the rules," Daniel argues. He had checked the Guild rules before making it his mission to help people in remote villages who couldn't afford to hire a huntsman.

"Do you accept any form of payment?" asks Huntmaster Eric Dillworth.

"Only lodging and food where appropriate," says Daniel, fighting the urge to explain more.

"Why should he?" Pine asks. "His Saroth wife was a Castaloni. She probably left him a fortune when she died."

Was murdered.

Daniel silently corrects Pine's statement, and his hands become fists at his sides. He concentrates on breathing slowly to give the anger time to fade.

"Why did we never receive anything?" inquires Lord Frederick Marsh, perking up at the mention of money. "Your contract requires you to donate a portion of any unexpected bounty."

Blood rushes to Daniel's face, making him hot and giving him a headache.

"Because there was no bounty from my wife's death." He spits the words with disgust. "Everything was put in trust for our daughter."

"Convenient," says Pine.

Lord Marsh sits back, losing interest.

"Let us return to the main point." Jordan sounds weary.

"Huntsman Daniel, please describe these non-Guild missions and your reason for accepting them when there are dozens of contracts available for a Seeker with your skills."

"The Guild contracts would take me away from my daughter for long periods of time," says Daniel. "I have not quit because I may wish to return to this life when Vic is old enough to be left alone or with a friend. These other voluntary jobs involve a variety of things: building, crafting, Seeking. Whatever people need but cannot afford."

"Where do you get the funds to do such noble work?" asks Pine. "That would hardly qualify as an expense for your daughter's benefit."

"Marina's father established several charity accounts," says Daniel. "She extended their use to me."

His stomach tightens with dread, recalling the outright lie he'd told Antonio Castaloni.

I'm sorry I couldn't protect her. I loved her with all my heart, and I still failed her.

The Council members debate amongst themselves for a while.

Lost in the misery of self-recrimination, Daniel lets their words wash over him without registering until Lord Terrence stands to deliver their conclusion.

"If you are agreeable, Huntsman Daniel, we have decided by a vote of four to three to offer you the option of choosing inactive Guild member status. This would require you to pay dues in full on the first day of each year and petition the Council before accepting any Guild contracts. You would be free to retain your rank and status as a huntsman and use your Gifts as you see fit."

Daniel knows they really couldn't stop him anyway, but he appreciates the gesture of formal permission.

"Do you accept these terms?" asks Jordan.

"I do." Daniel bows to the High Council before exiting, feeling oddly good about the outcome.

Chapter 17:
Tragic Accident

Cave on Mount Kaleri, Desolate Mountains
Five years and ten months after Marina's death
(Vic is six and a half years old)

Tielle knows something's wrong the instant she opens her eyes to complete darkness.

Stunned silence follows until Alec's voice breaks through the stillness.

"Mama!" His arms tighten around Tielle's neck.

"I'm here, baby." She releases her hold on Gabriel and returns Alec's fierce embrace.

A small fireball appears in Gabriel's left hand. His right still holds the Teleportation scroll.

"Where are we?" Tielle tries to speak calmly, but a tremor in her voice declares the fear.

Gabriel checks the scroll again, bringing the fireball as close as he dares and squinting at the destination line.

It keeps flickering, but there's not enough light to read what it says from Tielle's distance.

"I'm not sure. It keeps changing from Kartoff Mountains to Desolate Mountains," Gabriel reports grimly. He draws the second Teleportation scroll out from the inner pocket of his robes. As soon as he has it in hand, it disappears.

"Allow me to clarify," says a calm, contemptible, very familiar male voice. "You are in a dragon's cave midway up Mount Kaleri in the Desolate Mountains."

Gabriel steps left and pushes Tielle behind him.

Despite the terror running rampant through her, Tielle implements their emergency protocol. Conjuring a scroll with a containment shield, she sets Alec on his feet and forms the shield around him. It completes as dozens of torches flare to life around them, bathing them in soft orange light.

Panicked, Alec throws himself into the containment field, bounces off, and falls over. Leaping up, he charges forward and pounds his tiny fists into the field, face bright red with exertion.

Since Alec wears Gabriel's green Keeper's pendant, which has been imbued with a two-way communications spell linked to her pendant, Tielle activates the link. Her son's screams appear in her mind at full volume.

Kneeling, Tielle whispers to him.

"You're all right. I'm still here. Papa's still here. Calm down." Tielle presses both hands hard into the barrier, fighting rising panic.

Beside her, Gabriel's in wolf form, growling.

"What did you do?" Gabriel's question sounds menacing because of his current form.

Terrified, but not wanting Alec to hear the conversation, Tielle closes the link. Unsure if she has the strength to rise, she turns around and sits with her back to the containment field holding her son.

Gabriel's directly in front of her. The black fur along his back sticks straight up and every one of his lean, powerful muscles look ready for action.

Jackson stands about ten paces away. After exchanging their second Teleportation scroll for an illumination one, he releases three energy orbs. The brighter light reveals Jackson's triumphant expression. There's something strange and unnerving about his eyes.

"You should be more concerned with what you're going to do next to ensure your son has a future," says Jackson. "First, you're going to—"

Snarling, Gabriel leaps forward, closing the distance between them at a sprint. He slams into Jackson, but before they can hit the ground, the Conjurer vanishes.

Gabriel's hard landing stirs up a cloud of dust. The movement makes Tielle more aware of her surroundings. Piles of old bones litter the sandy cave floor. The area outlined in torches stretches left and right about twenty paces before starting to curve. There's a darkened area behind Jackson that neither the torches nor the energy orbs reach.

Only a pale purple light comes from fluorescent moss back there. It's enough to give her a rough estimate of the cavern's size but little more.

As she absorbs these details, a hand lands on Tielle's shoulder, and an oppressive weight presses down on her. She collapses onto her side, unable to move or breathe. The feeling vanishes as suddenly as it came, leaving her coughing and gasping.

Howling a challenge, Gabriel charges again.

This time, Jackson stretches out his left hand toward Gabriel.

Shock and horror shake Tielle as she watches her husband halt suddenly, then lay down with a low whimper.

"Are we done with this pointless fight yet?" asks Jackson.

Gabriel takes his human form but stays in a kneeling position. His green eyes shine with tears.

"You killed Marina, and you're here to kill us." Gabriel's voice lacks emotion. "Why, Jack?" He picks up some of the sand and lets it slip through his fingers.

"My Master would like a brief word with you, but I unfortunately have no fresh bodies for him to inhabit. He'll have to work through me. In that sense, it'll be like any Minder call. You'll have to accept his invitation to speak. Will you do that for me?"

Gabriel nods.

Tielle experiences the mental tug of a Minder wishing to connect. It's the equivalent of a polite knock upon a door. Needing answers, she accepts.

Jackson's eyes glow red.

The voice appearing in her mind sounds ancient, deep, and smooth.

Well met. You may call me the Dark Man. I apologize for what must be. You have something my faithful servant desires.

Confusion fills her until the spirit inhabiting Jackson's body pulls an image to the forefront of her thoughts.

A new pain stabs Tielle, stealing her breath.

"Alec!" His name is a prayer as it crosses her lips.

"No! Leave him!" cries Gabriel.

Lady Tielle, I need you to release the boy from the containment field.

Tielle casts a desperate look toward her husband. His expression projects frustration, but he neither moves nor speaks.

You and Gabriel will die soon. When that happens, the containment field could disappear or collapse. Do you wish to take that chance with the boy's life?

"No, but a sudden death might be more merciful than leaving him with you," says Tielle.

My servant cannot currently hear you, and you do not truly mean that. Consider the consequences if I must disappoint my servant. Your death and Gabriel's death will be slower. I may even have your sister and Lady Corabelle share your fate if you annoy me too much.

"Does Jackson love him?" Tielle wonders, aware every breath could be her last. "Will he take care of him?"

He does, and he will. Obedience comes with rewards. I have put the boy into a deep sleep, but I can lift the spell briefly for you and Gabriel to make peace with your child before ownership transfers to my servant. Do you agree to these terms, Lady Tielle?

In answer, Tielle breaks the containment field and crawls over to Alec. A sudden stream of tears blocks her vision of her son, but she's close enough to sit up and pull him onto her lap.

The next thing she's aware of is Gabriel's arms wrapped around both of them.

She doesn't know what conversation Gabriel had with the dark spirit, but his desperation comes through his embrace.

"Did you have a nice chat with my master?" asks Jackson.

"Jack, let them go," says Gabriel. "They're not a threat to you. Take the inheritance. Take everything. Don't go through with this. It's madness."

"I can't. You're both sponsors for Victoria," explains Jackson, "and if either of you live, you would have a claim to Alec as his parents."

"How many people have to die before you're satisfied?" Tielle wonders, settling into a numb state of acceptance.

"Well, at least one more beyond you," says Jackson. "The young Conjurer who created that Teleportation scroll for me." He gestures to the fallen scroll, which sits a few feet to their left. "She'll be so overcome with remorse by her mistake that she cannot bear living."

"I'm sure you have a hold over her," Gabriel says bitterly. "If it was enough to gain her cooperation, it should be enough to buy her silence."

"The surest silence is death," Jackson comments. "Now finish your farewells so we can move to the next step."

"Mama?" The dreamy quality disappears in Alec's next statement. "Don't leave me!" Once again, he clings hard to Tielle's neck.

Squeezing her eyes shut, she tries to memorize the moment. Tielle inhales deeply, heart breaking at the familiar scents of soap, dirt, and sweat. Remembering Gabriel, she breaks out of Alec's hold and transfers him to her husband. She glares at Jackson.

"If you want our son, listen closely." Her words flow out on a wave of anger. "He gets nightmares almost every night. Rubbing his back makes him feel better. He needs an energy orb near him to even fall asleep. He's allergic to peanuts but every other nut we've given him has been fine. He hasn't yet shown obvious signs of being a Conjurer, Destroyer, or Shapeshifter. My guess is he'll manifest Minder Gifts soon."

"Love him, and I mean that as a person, not as a means to an end," Gabriel adds.

"What end do you seek anyway?" Tielle asks. "Alec will never inherit while Victoria lives, and she is protected by something far greater than you or your master. She has the Lady's grace upon her."

"She is only half-Saroth," Jackson explains. "Alec is wholly Saroth. As long as he has some magical Gifts, the house council will have to heed his claim."

"What if that's not something he wants?" asks Gabriel.

"He will," Jackson counters. "I will teach him to claim what's rightfully his."

Tielle shudders and leans back against Gabriel, instinctively reaching for her son's hand.

He watches her intently.

She touches his cheek, treasuring the soft, warm skin beneath her fingertips.

"I only pray he never becomes like you," says Gabriel. He lets two beats pass. "What happens now? How are you going to do it? What will you tell Mother?"

"Don't do this," Tielle begs. "She's been through enough."

Your father. Your sister. Now us.

"Are you going to tell her the truth?" asks Gabriel.

"A version of it," says Jackson. "You had a terrible accident with a Teleportation scroll. It dropped you in the middle of a dragon's lair. I caught the mistake too late to save you, but I managed to conjure Alec to safety." He holds out both arms. "Give me the child."

Leaning across Gabriel, Tielle kisses Alec's forehead, cheeks, and nose, eliciting a giggle. The light, merry sound doesn't fit this grim place, but she forces a smile she doesn't feel.

"You're going on an adventure now with your Uncle Jack," says Gabriel. "Be our brave boy."

"We love you, Alec." Tielle's voice catches on his name. Fresh tears form. "And we always will."

Watching Alec stumble over to Jackson exhausts Tielle. Her heart fires several wordless prayers that her mind's too distraught to fashion properly.

Jackson picks up Alec.

The last thing Tielle sees of her son is his head lolling against Jackson's chest.

"I'm going to stay until the end, but don't worry about Alec," says Jackson. He backs into the deep shadows beyond the pool of light. "He will remember none of this. I promise."

Something large moves behind Jackson. A pair of bright orange and red eyes appear in the darkness. They rise up until they tower over Jackson's head.

For an instant, Tielle imagines the dragon will kill Jackson, righting many wrongs.

Instead, the beast shuffles around him and lumbers into the light. Its skull is massive and filled with many spikes. A trail of spikes flows down its back. Massive, leathery wings are tucked against its sides. If the creature opened its wings within the cavern, it might come close to brushing both walls at once.

It's a terrifying sight, but Tielle refuses to let it be the last vision she sees.

Tearing her gaze away from the dragon, Tielle seizes Gabriel's shirt and pulls him into a deep kiss.

"You're a Shapeshifter. You can fly," she declares. "Leave. Save Alec."

He tightens his hold on her, leaning his forehead upon hers.

"We will face this together."

Chapter 18:
Sign

North Library, Castaloni Estate, City of Dominance
Five days later (Five years and ten months after Marina's death)
(Vic is six and a half years old)

As he enters the library, Jackson pauses to observe his mother. Her long, graying black hair hangs loose, falling in haphazard waves past her shoulders. She slouches in a large reading chair, leaning her head on her right hand. Her eyes are directed into the middle of the fancy carpet, but Jackson knows she's not seeing much. He considers pushing the meeting off, but they already lost a few days. His mother had refused to see anybody besides Alec since the joint celebration of life ceremony the day after the tragic accident.

At least she's dressed and out of her room.

The servants he paid for timely information kept him apprised of Mother's condition. She'd fainted the moment Jackson broke the news to her. The rest of that day and the next, she had spent every waking moment with Alec. The servants barely got her to eat or drink anything until right before the ceremony. The days following have seen gradual improvements, but there's still a towel clutched in her left hand, ready to sop up more tears.

Jackson had always suspected Gabriel of being the favorite child. His mother's strong reaction to losing him only proves the point. She had cried over Marina's death but nothing like this.

No refusing food. No lengthy catatonic states.

He's offended on his sister's behalf.

Do not judge your mother too harshly. The immediate danger

to Victoria forced her to show strength while bearing the loss of her firstborn. No such immediacy occupies her attention this time since Alec is not yet the heir. This fragile state provides the perfect emotional ground for this discussion. Mika will be along shortly. Set the privacy spell and give her the tea.

Can you force her to sign the contract?

Conjuring a privacy scroll, Jackson activates it and tucks it under the chair his mother occupies.

We must discover her current thoughts and work within them. Anything your mother completely opposes will eventually reassert itself within her mind and be reversed accordingly. Suggest the idea of making Alec heir to the Castaloni fortune, but do not press the point today. This meeting is about becoming his guardian and making Victoria vulnerable.

A table sits next to the reading chair. Jackson finally notes that the table holds an odd collection of objects: a hairbrush, a Keeper's pendant, a small piece of bread, a memory crystal, and a ragged stuffed wolf. The toy and Keeper's pendant had belonged to Gabriel. He assumes the bread and hairbrush have something to do with Tielle. The memory crystal could be anything.

Curious, Jackson pulls the memory crystal to his hand and closes his eyes, letting the magic recreate the scene preserved inside. A crowded room appears in his mind's eye. In the distance, a dark-haired boy calmly walks out onto a stage. Jackson cuts the scene off and returns the memory crystal to the table. He doesn't need to see it. He was there in that miserably hot room, suffocating inside stiff formal robes while his brother cycled his forms to prove he was ready for intermediate studies in the Shapeshifter arts.

Why didn't Gabriel get a private tutor like the rest of us?

Your parents saw that he enjoyed being around people more than you or your sister. Training with other children fit him better.

Accepting his master's explanation, Jackson conjures a pot of tea and a cup, pours some for his mother, and delivers it before making room on the table for the pot. The towel she had been holding is damp, so he switches it out for a dry one, which he places near her left arm.

His mother sits up straighter and accepts the cup with two hands, but she does nothing with it except rest it on her lap.

Get her to drink the tea.

Suppressing the urge to sigh, Jackson pries the cup free and lifts it to his mother's lips.

"Drink this." He keeps the order calm and even. "It will make you feel better."

"I don't want to feel better." Despite the protest, his mother swallows some of the hot liquid. "I would much rather the pain end." Tears spill out onto her cheeks.

We can work with that if you like.

We are not killing my mother! You said we need her as a stabilizing force.

I stand by that, but nobody would question a suicide right now. The businesses should be able to absorb both blows. It may be better overall than spreading out the destruction, but I am merely making you aware of your options. Do with the information what you will as long as you accomplish my goal. Victoria is already six years old. She will be harder to deal with once she manifests magical Gifts. I want her eliminated.

While Jackson cannot understand why his master fears his niece so much, he learned long ago to let the Master rant at will, especially when playing host. The physical discomfort had ceased bothering him, but each instance left him wearier than the last.

You will need to practice calling my full essence from the Veil soon. My ability to shield your body from the effects of hosting my power is reaching its limits. But do not concern yourself with that now. Mika has arrived.

Jackson turns in time to watch the counselor and purser enter the room and shut the door. The man lingers with his right palm resting on the door. Being connected to the Master lets Jackson sense the moment the barrier seals the room. It's wasteful, but Jackson waits patiently while Mika Forester seals off the library's second entrance, which leads to a sitting room. He had assured the counselor the servants would not disturb them, but given the man's fickle loyalties, Jackson really can't blame him for being paranoid.

Can we trust him?

More than most. Less than some.

What does that mean?

He grew up with your father. They were very close friends. That is a mark against us as Mika is aware of your part in Antonio's death.

Once finished, the counselor crosses over to Jackson's mother, kisses her left cheek, and works his way through the expected sympathetic nonsense.

Jackson tunes the man out in favor of learning more about him. *How did he learn about that?*

Your sister told him when they were modifying provisions in her will. They had a privacy spell up, but I was with him at the time. Mika may not be a whole-hearted servant like you, but he is a practical soul with genuine contempt for those who break social barriers.

Instead of describing the man's reasons with words, the Master transfers the knowledge directly to Jackson. Mika's parents—Ariella Puchini and Carlo Forester—had a whirlwind romance. Though she was the fourth of six children, Ariella hailed from one of the most prominent families in Saroth society. They had built more than half the buildings in Dominance. The moderately wealthy Forester family supplied the lumber for those projects. Their sudden marriage was not received well by either family, leading to Ariella being cut off from her family. The stress led to strife which turned to tragedy before Mika's eighth birthday when his father killed his mother and himself. Knowing of the friendship between Antonio and Mika, the Castalonis had taken the orphan into their home.

Rational or not, his history makes him wary of those who leap to higher social strata. Your mother did precisely that. I believe Mika's disagreement over Antonio courting her may have been the greatest strain their relationship ever bore. He loved your father like a brother and will defend the house interests to the bitter end, regardless of the heir's identity. That makes him an ally.

Jackson watches the counselor interact with his mother. The man's every gesture conveys compassion, despite bearing some responsibility for the pain she endures. Once again, Jackson questions the wisdom of their deal. In short, to get around Marina's many conditions, Mika would assume the duties of running the holdings in Jackson's stead.

Is he a trustworthy puppet? He has betrayed Mother. He could betray us.

You raise a valid point. If it comes to that, he also has a wife, two children, and several grandchildren to threaten, but so far, I have found him competent and reasonable. The pleasantries have completed. It is time to listen.

"I'm sorry to bother you with business now, but we must settle Gabriel's affairs quickly since there is a child involved," says Mika. "Your son passed without modifying his will in several years. The boy inherits everything from him and from the mother, but each stated the other as guardian and caretaker."

"I will raise him," says Mother.

Jackson's pleased to see she looks more alert.

"Are you sure that is wise, my lady?" asks Mika. "He will have enemies because of his name. Are you certain you wish to add those who oppose the Tariku League to that list?"

"I can protect him." Mother's voice increases in strength as she continues, "I'll hire a team of personal guards if necessary." Her determined expression adds a silent declaration about knowing how to raise children to adulthood, which is true.

Jackson and his siblings suffered no hardships while growing up, even with the inherent dangers of their house name.

They would still be alive if not for me.

Guilt flutters in Jackson's stomach, but he dismisses it.

They chose the wrong master. I deserve the power I've worked for.

"That will be fine while he's a small child," says Mika, "but what happens when he becomes a young man? Constant supervision can be constricting. I know this from experience. A failed assassination attempt on Antonio's mother forced the entire household to stay indoors for almost a month. It was awful."

He has prepared the way well. Offer your alternative.

"I can spare him from that fate," says Jackson. He waits until the words capture his mother's attention. "Make me Alec's guardian, and I will make him my apprentice and heir. My servants can watch him and care for his current needs. When he is old enough, I will train him. If he shows a Gift other than Conjuring, we can obtain a proper tutor or send him to study at the Alamon Temple as Marina did."

Mika pretends to consider the proposal for the first time before agreeing.

"It's a good plan," Mika says, addressing them equally before facing Jackson. "Do you have a contract prepared?"

Jackson conjures the contract they created together several weeks ago and hands it to his mother for inspection.

She studies the terms carefully, as Jackson knew she would, but eventually, she conjures an ink well and quill and signs the contract, giving Jackson custody of Alec.

Once Mika verifies and witnesses the signature, Jackson tucks the contract into the Veil.

"Not every guard must be visible," Mother points out, sending the writing implements away. "Few of Victoria's watchers even hold the title, but if this can offer Alec more freedom and keep him safe, I support it."

"That is another matter I meant to raise, my lady," says Mika. "The tax laws recently changed. Those in favor of Saroth isolation from the wider world have won a great victory. We can no longer cover the expense of guards for Victoria without facing severe penalties. This would not be so if she lived within Caramore's borders."

"Daniel would never agree to the condition," says Mother, "but I can hire private guards to replace company ones if that's easier for you."

"You may find that difficult. The Arkonai have petitioned for the right to tax those who work in lands protected by the Guild," Mika explains. "The Tariku League has agreed to the condition in exchange for the Arkonai maintaining a presence in Fort Merit and Fort Knowledge. That would cut down on the area the Shadow Army needs to patrol and discourage dragons from venturing outside the Ashlands and the Badlands."

Mother accepts this news in stride.

"Then I will hire huntsmen or give Daniel the means to do so."

Mika sends Jackson a questioning look. They had not anticipated this much resistance on the point.

The Dark Man chuckles.

Apparently, we need to be clearer. Call forth the second contract.

Jackson does so while Mika explains.

"This is a contract in which you agree to recall every person sent to safeguard Victoria from afar."

"Why would I endanger my granddaughter?" asks Mother, glaring at the counselor.

"To save your grandson," Mika answers softly. "Take the contract and sign it. The details are inside."

Mother starts to rise, but Jackson's left hand flies out with the Dark Man's power flowing through him.

"Sign." Jackson doesn't recognize his own voice. He holds out the contract, gives her a pre-inked quill, and creates a flat surface with his hands to ease the process.

A strange, dazed look sweeps over his mother. She signs then loses consciousness.

I thought you said mind control wouldn't work.

I said it wouldn't work forever. She will eventually

remember removing Victoria's protections and try to right things. Mika will give her false reports to delay that inevitability. It should expand our time for planning. With the proper distractions, it may even last years. Keep your time with her to a minimum. If she ever brings it up, focus on the contract made for Alec.

Chapter 19:
Destroyer Gifts

Marina's Final Resting Place, Karnok Mountains
Eight years after Marina's death
(Vic is almost nine years old)

Eight years without you.

Daniel sits before the small, pristine headstone. It hasn't changed much in appearance since the day they laid it in place and imbued it with memories and protective enchantments. Marcus said Navina had stopped by last week to renew the enchantments and add some new memories, but Daniel had been too busy preparing for a visit from Tellen and Katrina to experience them.

Eager to see what surprises Marcus has arranged this time, Daniel lays his hand on the right side as instructed to access only the new memories. Closing his eyes, he sees a clear image of Marina holding a fireball in her left hand and leaning over to check a dark corner of their apartment in Temperance. Knowing what comes next, he laughs. As the fire approaches the hole, hundreds of spiders burst forth and scatter. Startled, Marina shrieks and stumbles back. The memory fades, but Daniel remembers catching her. He lifts his hand off the headstone to ponder what happened next.

He had offered to kill the spiders, but Marina wouldn't let him. Instead, she had hired a Conjurer to clear out any unwanted lifeforms and relocate them to the Silver Springs Forest. Daniel's thoughts linger on the three weeks they spent camping on the Plains of Forgiveness before moving into the apartment. Danger of discovery made them vigilant, as Christa had not yet cleared them of her uncle's murder, but the long nights alone beneath a host of stars had bound them together in unexpected ways.

Those days and nights were perfect. I wanted them to go on forever.

The only major close call happened when a Shapeshifter master and apprentice had stumbled across their campsite. Daniel recalls drawing a bow and arrow from the Veil, ready to kill one of the majestic deer. It would have provided food for several weeks. Marina had not only stopped him but also taught him something about his Seeker Gifts. Ordinary animals and Shapeshifters feel different when he Seeks them. She said the knowledge likely unfolded differently for the various magic schools. To her, as a former Destroyer, it felt like the difference between torchlight and the pure white light of an energy orb. Tielle had once described it as magic currents. Since Daniel has no better explanation, he accepts these answers.

He tries to halt the thoughts there but remembers asking Marina if her people feared accidentally killing a Shapeshifter. Her reply had haunted him then and still makes him uneasy.

Accidental deaths are rare because basic Shapeshifter training hones a keen sense of danger, prompting a shift to a new form any time there's a threat. However, certain people target Shapeshifters, trying to murder them in an animal form under the assumption that consuming them can harness some of their magic.

If we don't have enough ways to hurt each other, we invent more.

Heart heavy, Daniel touches the headstone again and waits for the second memory. It shows him Marina in a storage room surrounded by herbs, pointing out a few and explaining something about them. He gathers that the memory came from Raelyn and wonders how long Marcus has had it.

He must have planned this before the quest to save Vic.

The next image shows Marina kneeling before Huntmaster Garok. Despite the brevity, Daniel has heard Callen tell the story enough times to grasp the significance. In that moment, his beautiful, brave, dangerously reckless wife had surrendered to a madman so Callen's family would be spared.

The fourth memory unfolds as a scene, complete with vivid details. Daniel is transported back into Aridel's Northgate Prison, watching Marcus's first meeting with Marina. The Minder had been asking to break the marriage contract set up between them to unite the Polani and Castaloni houses. Ironically, the mission to find and save Marina brought Marcus close to his true love, Gabriella.

Even without trying, you brought people together.

As if to prove his point, the next scene shows Marina laughing. Daniel recognizes the table in one of Christa's drawing rooms. The presence of Annie and cards tells him they're likely in the middle of a round of Challenger or some other group game. He wonders how Marina fared against Christa in the card game. His childhood friend had been ruthless when they'd played for shiny stones and sweets stolen from the kitchen while the cook wasn't looking.

The sixth image features Marina sleeping in a rocking chair with the infant version of Vic slung across her chest. Daniel lifts his hand, wanting to let that memory stay with him. Guilt creeps in. He'd interrupted that sweet scene by waking Marina so she could make it to a meeting with the Castaloni house council followed by another meeting with the regional managers. It had been the first day back to reality after the blissful haze of Vic's first month of life.

"She's changed over the years," he murmurs. The statement prompts Daniel to think about his daughter. "But she's a lot like you."

Vic's blond hair likely comes from his parents, as it's lighter than his brown hair, but nearly every other physical feature channels more of Marina than him. But the similarities go far deeper than Vic and Marina having the same shade of eye color. Vic has her mother's curiosity, the need to wander and explore, and a love of learning new things.

After playing the original memories by touching the left side, Daniel gets up.

"I'll be thinking of you," he promises, "but I have a camping trip to run tonight for the children. Vic's been eager for company. Katrina and Tellen visit when they can, but they spend a lot of time training."

He frowns, wondering whether he should air his concerns and feeling foolish for worrying.

"She hasn't shown any more signs of magic since the attack years ago," he says. "None from an identifiable school anyway. That light may have come from the bracers, not her. It may mean Vic is Bereft. I'll love her regardless, but I'm hoping she has magic. I want her to fit in somewhere. I've taught her how to survive in the forest, but someday, she will face people and their faults, schemes, and prejudices. I don't know how to prepare her for that."

Daniel mulls over the issue while walking back to his cabin.

Do we misunderstand magic? Can people Gifted in one area train in powers from other schools?

When Marina lost her Destroyer powers, she was able to

manifest something very close to Healer Gifts, even if she could never control the timing.

"Papa! Look what Tellen can do!"

Daniel spots Vic and Tellen standing by the stump he uses to split firewood. His daughter shakes with excitement. Tellen remains calm but also appears pleased. Daniel doesn't see Katrina, but a check with his Seeker Gifts confirms the Shapeshifter is in beetle form sitting on top of the woodpile.

Placing a fresh log on the stump, Tellen backs up a step and waves for Vic to retreat as well. Once she moves to a safe distance, the boy closes his eyes and bows his head.

The log rocks slightly, but otherwise nothing happens.

As Daniel opens his mouth to question what he's seeing, a loud crack sounds and the log tumbles from the stump in three neat sections.

Vic cheers.

"It's amazing! Can you do it again?"

"I think there's enough firewood," Daniel says, noticing the sweat along Tellen's brow. The number of pieces around the stump indicates that he has not witnessed the second demonstration or even the third.

More like fourth or fifth.

"But you said we need some for the trip," Vic argues.

"We can gather what we need when we reach the campsite," says Daniel.

"Can't you put some extra in the Veil, so we don't have to gather it later?" Vic asks.

"The Veil should not be used for everyday storage needs," Daniel points out, trying not to smile.

"It would be bad to need a sword and end up drawing a piece of wood," Tellen explains. "Some huntsmen can't access the Veil and others who can don't bother. They prefer carrying their weapons."

"Doesn't that get heavy?" asks Katrina, having returned to human form.

"I guess, but high stamina and great strength can be part of a Guardian's Gifts," Tellen answers.

"Those who choose not to use the Veil tend to have a preferred weapon type," says Daniel.

"Or can only use one weapon," Tellen adds.

Vic casts a curious look at Tellen.

"I thought Guardian Gifts were about fighting and protecting," she says. "How come you can split logs? It doesn't sound like a Guardian Gift."

"That's because it's not," Katrina answers. "It's probably a form of deconstruction. That's a Destroyer power."

"I'm not a Destroyer," Tellen declares.

Daniel holds out his hands to stop the debate.

"We can discuss this more later. Go grab your packs. We need to leave to reach the campsite by dark."

Since everything has been packed ahead of time, this process doesn't take long. The children each bear appropriately sized bundles containing blankets and food. Ducking into the cabin, Daniel picks up his bag, which contains a blanket, a comb for Vic, more food, utensils, and a cooking pot to expand their meal options beyond freshly killed meat cooked over open flames.

They start walking along the trail Daniel mapped out earlier.

Katrina's okay with meat, right?

Daniel directs the thought to Marcus. The reply isn't instant like it was in days gone by, but he eventually receives an amused answer.

Certainly. One of her forms is a dog. They eat meat.

Good. I just assumed Shapeshifters might be more sympathetic to small creatures.

The Saroth who avoid meat tend to be related to a Shapeshifter who becomes a small woodland creature. Most Shapeshifters have at least one carnivorous form and will happily devour anything their animal form would naturally consume. Any other burning questions before I go? I have to meet the Council in a few minutes to give a long-winded, boring report.

You do that. I'll be herding three bickering young people through the Karnok Mountains.

Tell Katrina I love her.

"Katrina, your father says he loves you!" Daniel calls.

The announcement ends the current debate.

Caught off guard, Katrina inclines her head, cheeks reddening.

She said she loves you too. Daniel lies.

Really? I heard 'Stop embarrassing me.'

I might have taken liberties with interpreting the look she gave in response. If you don't like the interpretation, don't make me the middleman.

Marcus's laughter fills Daniel's mind before tapering off into the sense of a sad smile.

Take care of my baby girl, Daniel.

She's flying circles around us, but I shall do my best to keep up with her.

Daniel doesn't feel the connection end, but he assumes Marcus's attention is elsewhere when he doesn't get a response. The hike turns into a mostly pleasant affair. Tellen keeps to a steady, even pace without complaint. Katrina adjusts her pack and takes dog form whenever she grows weary of walking normally. Not having the benefit of long training or the ability to change forms, Vic lags behind, occasionally complaining about sore feet.

Maybe she's too young for such a long hike.

Daniel relieves Vic of her pack but makes no other concessions to her complaints.

Eventually, when nobody responds, Vic stops voicing them.

When they arrive at the campsite, Daniel pulls the waterbags from the Veil, instructs everybody to drink their fill, then sends Katrina and Vic to refill them in the nearby stream while he and Tellen tend to other camp duties. While they're alone, Daniel asks the question that occurred to him during the hike.

"Do you want me to find a master to help you understand the Destroyer Gifts?"

"I'm not a Destroyer," Tellen protests by reflex.

"I'm not saying you are, but if you want to use that portion of your magical abilities, you will need to train in it like any other skill," Daniel says. "You have tutors for swordplay, archery, and wielding daggers. This is no different."

He stops talking before he can subject the boy to the full version of his magic-schools-are-myths speech.

Daniel finishes laying out the blankets and arranging a firepit, letting the boy think about the offer. As he despairs of getting an answer, Tellen speaks.

"Master Daniel, can I show you something?"

Receiving a nod, Tellen draws out the daggers always sheathed at his waist. Facing a large tree, Tellen focuses on the daggers.

A thin stream of lightning appears between the blades. Tellen pushes out with the dagger blades, flinging the little bolt into the tree. The boy turns to Daniel with mixed emotions moving across his face.

"I'm a Guardian," says Tellen, "but I want to learn to control this too." He sends two small sparks zipping along the edge of both daggers. "Can you help me?"

"Personally, no," Daniel admits, "but I know somebody who can find you the right master."

Chapter 20:
A Discreet Transaction

Lady Mekrian's House of Discreet Transactions, City of Temperance
Eight years and one week after Marina's death
(Vic is almost nine years old)

Corabelle rises as Daniel enters the room. He bows, and she waves for him to be seated.

"Thank you for meeting with me," says Daniel, sitting stiffly in the chair. He reaches for the cup set before him.

"You probably shouldn't drink that unless you've read the room's history and verified it's safe," Corabelle says. "Even then, you're better off accessing a waterbag you've prepared yourself. This isn't one of the rooms designed to block your Seeker abilities. You should have access to the Veil."

She waits while Daniel wraps his fingers around the cup and follows the advice of applying his Gifts to peek into the recent past. Since she had arrived only a few minutes before him and the drink was warm when she got there, Corabelle knows the reading won't take too long.

"Something's been added to the drink, though I can't tell what it is or why it was added," Daniel reports.

"It's common practice to add calming agents to drinks in places like this," Corabelle explains, glancing up to indicate the whole establishment. "Calm people tend to kill each other less when their meetings go awry. If you trust me, I can conjure something else for you. Do you have a preference for food or drink?"

When he doesn't answer right away, she conjures a pitcher and two clear glasses. Leaning forward, Corabelle pours the water. Sipping from one she slides the other toward Daniel.

He catches it but merely fingers the sweat beading on the side, watching her with concern.

"Are you safe, my lady?" he asks.

"There are no current threats worth mentioning," Corabelle answers. "Marcus has recently obtained the position of Spymaster. His office oversees many things, including the safety of Tariku League members. I believe I'm in good hands. What about you and Victoria? Have you been training her?"

Daniel's mood brightens at the mention of his daughter.

"Vic can handle a sword well for her age," he says. "And her tracking skills are improving. Her stamina on long hikes needs work, and she lacks the patience for traditional hunts. But she can catch a fish if she needs to and hit stationary targets with throwing daggers or arrows."

The worried expression returns to Daniel.

"What concerns do you have?" Corabelle prompts. "Is Victoria hurt? Ill?" She holds in the other half-dozen fears.

"Nothing like that," Daniel assures her. "I don't think Vic's ever been ill. I assumed it was her bracers at work."

Corabelle relaxes slightly.

"Has she shown signs of Destroyer Gifts?" Corabelle thinks of the vague request she got to search for available masters. She likes the idea of her granddaughter possessing Gifts from the same school of magic as her daughter.

Shaking his head, Daniel frowns.

"Vic has shown very little signs of any magic," he says. "A few times she's started glowing or shining light like she did during that attack when she was three but nothing more."

"Some people discover their Gifts later," says Corabelle.

"I would worry less if I knew she could defend herself without those bracers." Daniel rotates the water glass so fresh condensation faces him.

"You didn't come here to discuss Victoria's lack of magic, so what is this about?"

Daniel goes quiet for several beats before shaking off the melancholy mood.

"It's about Tellen. He's the son of Ireena and Callen. Marina met them in New Haven."

Although she controls the urge to flinch, Corabelle cannot stop the waves of sorrow and anger the memory prompts. She wasn't there, but she had seen enough horrors in the Vision Cast from the Observatory and witnessed the aftermath. An image of her firstborn bound to a pole and surrounded by Arkonai Brotherhood men chills her. The subsequent memory of sitting by Marina's bed as she recovered from the horrific experience gives the sorrow a stronger edge.

"Marcus mentioned you had unofficially taken over some of the boy's combat training," says Corabelle, hoping it's enough to get Daniel to elaborate.

"He's most proficient with daggers, but most huntsmen undergo extensive training with other weapon types," Daniel explains.

"I thought huntsmen usually train in larger schools," says Corabelle.

"He did for a time," says Daniel, "but during this past year, Tellen had some trouble at school. He should have gained a Guardian master by now since most of his Gifts align with that school, but many have chosen other apprentices and the rest—"

"Are afraid to train him because he has Destroyer Gifts," Corabelle finishes, summing up the problem. "Their fears are justified. Untrained Destroyers can be very destructive. Antonio and I hired a master for Marina at the first signs of her Gifts, but it took almost two years of training before she gained enough control to keep from releasing random bolts of lightning." Corabelle recalls having to save quite a few curtains and repair several couches from lightning accidents.

"Did your inquiries yield any results?" asks Daniel.

"Some, but I need to ask you some pointed questions before I can make a recommendation," says Corabelle. The detail of the potential student being Arkonai complicates matters. She discards half the candidates, knowing they wouldn't take the job anyway based on their situations or prejudices.

"Do you have permission to speak for the boy and his parents?" asks Corabelle. She pauses long enough to receive Daniel's nod. "What are his views on being trained by a woman?"

"He has had female teachers before," Daniel says defensively.

"This isn't a class setting." Corabelle lets the reminder sink in a second. "The tutoring would likely have to be run in a place like this. Despite my efforts, the Tariku League has been making it harder for people to work or trade outside of Caramore or Kaltan City."

At first, the changes had hurt the shipping, storage, and scroll-making businesses, but eventually, Mika Forester turned things around by exploiting loopholes in the laws. Though her personal distrust of the man has increased, Corabelle respects his ability to run the holdings in Jackson's name.

"It might even be necessary to conduct the lessons under a privacy spell," she adds, thinking aloud. "He wouldn't be able to explain what went on during the sessions, but the knowledge and skills gained would remain his forever."

"Why would that be necessary?" Daniel wonders.

"Because Saroth society is as broken as yours, Daniel," says Corabelle. "Anybody I ask to do this would be looked down upon by their neighbors. The consequences could get much worse than scorn very quickly. Some view the training process with religious fervor, and they have very narrow definitions about who is worthy of the knowledge."

"That's madness," says Daniel.

"Your people have the Resolute and the Arkonai Brotherhood. We have the Purists and several other similar organizations." Corabelle drinks some of the water and studies the remaining clear liquid. "There are times to take direct action and times to work within the system we're given. I believe this is the latter case."

"How much will it cost?" Daniel inquires. "Callen and Ireena have set aside some money and given me permission to negotiate on their behalf. I can have the coins exchanged or converted to pure metal."

"There cannot be direct compensation without creating a legal mess," Corabelle explains. "Both councils would want to dictate what the master teaches and be paid for the privilege of meddling, but I do still have a possibility to discuss with you."

Daniel leans forward to show his interest.

"Abriel Candera was Marina's master for more than a decade." Aside from the brief Minder messages to gauge her interest in this mysterious job, Corabelle hasn't spoken to the short, fiery, dark-skinned woman since Marina dropped her Destroyer studies to learn healing techniques at the Alamon Temple. "She's retired and would probably enjoy the challenge."

Daniel fires questions about Master Candera's qualifications and experience, and Corabelle fields them with ease. If this works, she will set her people to discovering the lady's favorite wine, food, and other small comforts. She doesn't bother explaining this to Daniel. Many a grander transaction has been settled for favors and gifts. That's why places like Lady Mekrian's House of Discreet Transactions exist.

They swiftly work out the details of the basic contract, which outlines the deal in extremely vague terms. It confirms that Daniel has been chosen to pursue a trainer for Tellen and that Corabelle will help him find somebody appropriate. They set up a new meeting in three days to bring the two parties together for further discussion. If both agree, training can begin immediately and continue as long as necessary. Any future meetings would be up to the master and student to arrange.

As soon as they close out that business, Corabelle conjures two scrolls and offers them to Daniel.

"These are for Victoria. Please see that she receives them. One contains a fireworks display. Please use it in an open field. The other contains some stories she may enjoy if she likes reading." Not knowing the answer to that simple question bothers Corabelle. She should be able to visit her granddaughter and learn everything that matters to the child.

Daniel rises, thanks her, and tucks the scrolls into the Veil, promising to complete the delivery later.

A sudden longing to see Victoria strikes Corabelle, but she resists the urge to ask Daniel to bring the girl to their next meeting.

Keeping her distant keeps her safe.

Corabelle's not entirely convinced by this notion, but she can't argue with the fact that Victoria and Daniel have enjoyed several years of peace. Once the girl nears the age of majority, they can broach the subject of Victoria moving to Caramore and studying to accept her inheritance.

She may not even desire the power, position, or wealth.

Marina had been very reluctant to take on the responsibilities.

It might be better if Victoria never knows of the possibility.

"Is she happy?" asks Corabelle.

The question startles her and Daniel.

"What do you mean?" Daniel wonders.

Raising a hand to beg for patience, Corabelle tries to organize her roiling thoughts.

"Marina's wealth belongs to Victoria—and you—with no expectations." Corabelle sends Daniel a faint smile. "Given the way you spend money, it would last several lifetimes."

"We don't need it," says Daniel. "I've withdrawn some of the money to get Vic clothes, but otherwise, I can work or trade for things we don't have. We won't go hungry if that's your main concern."

Corabelle shakes her head, frustrated by the inability to explain her thoughts. She lowers her hand and studies it, noticing wrinkles lining the back. She forms a fist to temporarily vanquish the wrinkles.

"I didn't come from wealth, so I understand happiness isn't linked directly to its presence or absence." She meets Daniel's steady gaze. "I married a good man who happened to be wealthy. We built a life together, but it was not an easy transition for me, going from invisible to the center of attention."

Nobody knows you. Then everybody knows your name and has an opinion on how you look, dress, think, and act. Can Victoria handle that kind of attention?

"I'm happy to keep things as they are and reveal the inheritance to Victoria in time, but if you wish, I can also release her from the burden."

Silence falls as Daniel weighs Corabelle's proposal.

"What would that mean for her?" he inquires. "How could you accomplish it?"

"As Victoria's guardian, you can move to sell the businesses on her behalf," Corabelle explains. "Mika and Jackson would oppose you, but many managers would support the move. It would eventually be voted upon by the house council, and I can make that vote go any way you wish."

Daniel stares at the floor while he thinks.

Corabelle lets the silence remain.

"Let's leave things as they are," he says at last. "We still have seven years to decide. Vic can make that call when she's a woman." The last word puts an odd expression on Daniel's face, like he's never considered his daughter ever growing up completely.

They do grow up fast.

The conversation quickly closes. Daniel leaves, but Corabelle stays to think in peace. She doesn't visit such places regularly, but she sees the appeal of a few hours free of expectations and obligations. These places have a well-deserved shady reputation, but Corabelle enjoys being able to use the protections to accomplish something good.

The potential for good, evil, and everything in between under one roof. How convenient.

Chapter 21:
Purists and Prisoners

Temporary Camp, Karnok Mountains
Twelve years and four months after Marina's death
(Vic is thirteen years old)

"Where do you want us to stand, Exalted One?" asks the Purist Speaker.

Jackson can't remember this one's name until his master reminds him. He finds the title odd but admits he could get used to it.

Pietro Serco.

Any relation to Adaram?

Jackson's right hand forms a fist, which he imagines knocking into the Nokarti Assassin's face. He has been responsible for several plans failing over the past two decades. Jackson knows the accusation's not entirely fair. The real thorn is Marcus Polani. Even after they forced Mother to withdraw Victoria's protection, Marcus managed to keep people near her location. Whenever possible, he sent his daughter, Katrina, to stay with Victoria and Daniel. Thus, the guardians assigned to the Polani girl also became Victoria's silent saviors. That would no longer be a problem now that Katrina has reached the age of majority.

She has no protection today. We will succeed.

The magic bracers will strive to protect Victoria. Even without distinct magical gifts, she could be dangerous. Do not underestimate Tellen or the Polani girl. Both are fiercely loyal to Victoria. As for Pietro, he is Adaram's younger brother. You have been silent a while. You should answer the man.

"Surround them," Jackson orders, "but stand at least five paces away so you're not affected."

130

As one, the Purists make fists with their right hands and tap their chests three times in rapid succession, once for him and twice for the Dark Man.

While waiting for his help to move into position, Jackson surveys their captives. Each man or woman sits on the ground with their hands bound to their feet and wears a gag to preserve the peace. The Purists have brought him a well-rounded collection of prisoners today: six Arkonai, seven Bereft, and one Saroth traitor. Eight of the unfortunate souls came from Dawtan Prison in Temperance where two Purists were guards. Pietro earned the right to be Speaker by capturing a Saroth traitor and the man's Arkonai lover on the way to exchange vows at the Alamon Temple. The remaining prisoners came from Aridel, Outreach, Serene Hills, and Oldwick.

Both plans are in place. The fence has been weakened and the arrangements have been made. A servant has set up the nullifier field around this section of the Karnok Mountains to prevent Daniel's return for a time. Now, address the prisoners. You may not need the theatrics, but your followers will thrive on it.

"Today is an important day," says Jackson, scanning the crowd. "The Saroth people have hidden in Caramore far too long."

The Purists cheer.

"You are part of the change," Jackson declares. "Your bodies will join the Master's army and subdue the land. Though you are few today, your ranks will swell as the fighting spreads. What last words do you have to say?"

Starting left to right, Jackson gives each prisoner the chance to speak. The first two men use the time to curse him. The third man cries. The fourth through eighth men voice heartfelt pleas for their lives. The Purists jeer and mock in equal measures. Next, Jackson reaches the only woman. Her blond hair reminds him of Lady Christa, but the similarities end there. This lady looks scared beyond speech. She surprises him by turning to the Saroth traitor and declaring her love for him. Disappointed, Jackson replaces the gag and lets the traitor speak, preparing for another sappy declaration of love. Once again, he's surprised.

"The One's might and the Lady's grace will prevail," says the Saroth man, looking directly at Jackson. "Turn away from evil and do good."

The statement sounds like the nonsense Alec would utter. Jackson accidentally hired a governess who devoutly followed the One.

He had fired her as soon as he discovered what she was teaching the boy, but by then, she'd had three years to indoctrinate the child. The woman had even told Alec about his parents, Marina, Victoria, and so on through several branches of the Castaloni family. Jackson certainly wanted the boy to know such things, but he saw no point in burying the child in house history yet.

"Thank you for sharing that fine delusion," Jackson answers, returning his focus to the moment. He replaces the man's gag and moves on.

The others have nothing noteworthy to add, just more curses or pleas. The last man refuses to speak. He merely spits in Jackson's direction.

"I appreciate your contribution as well," says Jackson.

Shall I proceed with the ritual?

A warm sensation runs through Jackson's chest, letting him know he has the Master's approval. Despite having the spell memorized, Jackson conjures a scroll holding the words and unfurls it with a flourish. He sets it to hover slightly to his left at a good height for reading. Alarmed cries turn into a meaningless droning noise because of the gags. Stretching his hands out wide to encompass the whole group, Jackson begins speaking.

The first half of the spell focuses on drawing out the life energy from each captive. As the section completes, the prisoners have dazed looks and slump against each other. One of the Arkonai men from Temperance rallies enough strength to glare at Jackson before passing out.

The second half of the spell weaves the captives' souls together so that when they're released, they'll stay close enough to reanimate the bodies and be united to a single purpose.

Many years ago, they had sent zombies after Victoria, but since the force had consisted of a few small batches of random zombies, the creatures lacked coordination.

We will not repeat that mistake.

Jackson doesn't feel any change until he speaks the last word. The energy flow begins as a trickle, rejuvenating his senses. Previously, his arms had sagged from being stretched out for so long. When the trickle turns into a stream, his arms regain their strength. The next instant Jackson feels invincible.

You will need me to connect to each spirit.

You said that would be dangerous.

Danger or failure. Those are your options.

Accepting his master's words, Jackson braces for the painful connection. He doesn't feel any change until the Dark Man reaches through him to every soul there.

Master, the Purists!

The force isn't large enough. They must join the cause. Stop resisting. The energy must flow freely. Otherwise, the Saroth may live through the initial experience. That would be unpleasant for them.

Throughout the Master's speech, Jackson feels the energy build until his skin darkens and cracks. He clenches his eyes shut and screams long and loud enough to rip his throat raw. Even without sight, Jackson tracks the progress as the Master weaves throughout the souls scattered in the clearing. Faint cries of fear and dismay reach his ears. The souls gather closer together.

It is time.

Jackson releases the pent-up power.

A fire ignites in each body, instantly killing the Bereft, Arkonai, and two Saroth. The other Saroth scream and instinctively try to control the fire, but their pathetic efforts fail, overwhelmed by the supernatural power flowing through Jackson.

Turn away or your eyes will burn.

Jackson's body moves without conscious thought. Even with averted eyes and back turned to the blaze, spots of light dance before Jackson. The heat slams across his back. He staggers and leans on a tree to catch his balance. His left hand touches the bark then sinks into the tree as the power inside him burns through the section in contact with his hand. He doesn't need to see to know what is happening.

Create the portal.

Pushing past sudden weariness, Jackson turns again, raises both hands, and delivers the spell that will open the Darkland portal. Without sustained dark energy that can be found in the Badlands and Ashlands, the portal collapses almost immediately, but two Kaitid Spirits slip through and choose hosts from among the waking dead. The first Kaitid Spirit flows into the Arkonai woman, and the second chooses the Saroth traitor. The inky black Darkland spirits flow into the empty shells left behind by the cleansing fire.

Instruct them. I will be nearby in case something goes wrong.

As the Dark Man departs, Jackson opens his eyes to see the two skeletons sit up and clasp hands. Knowing that these undead would have their clothes, flesh, and hair burned away does not prepare Jackson adequately for the sight. The bones should also have been reduced to ashes, but the same power that protected Jackson also prevented the complete destruction of the bodies. He conjures fresh sets of rags and weapons collected over the years and drops the equipment in a heap before the zombies.

"Dress and arm," Jackson orders.

Why must they dress?

He indulges in the question because he has to wait for them to obey anyway.

The clothes will protect them same as they would a living being, making it harder for their enemies to return them to dust.

Jackson watches the progress without further comment. Seeing which weapon each chooses fascinates him. About half the zombies pick up swords or spears. Most of the rest sling quivers full of arrows across their backs and pick up bows. One selects a fine pair of daggers. The two possessed ones conjure long spirit swords. They look exactly like normal swords, except for the glint of supernatural energy flowing off them.

To Jackson's surprise, the armed zombies form four neat rows of five. It's eerie to see so many empty eyes set upon him. At the two ends of the first row stand the undead controlled by the Kaitid Spirits. Their eyes glow with strange blue light.

You may continue.

"About five miles from this point, there is a cabin hidden in this forest." Jackson points in the appropriate direction. "There you will find three people: a young Arkonai man, a young Saroth woman, and a child with the bloodlines of both magic races in her. Kill them."

The undead leaders step out of line and speak to the others in a language Jackson doesn't recognize. The words produce a burning sensation in his ears.

Leave them. They will obey. Seed the forest with other bands of zombies in case Victoria and her friends escape. Then return to Fort Medron and prepare another message for the Supreme Huntmaster. I will have another servant deliver it same as the first. Wear a cloak with a cowl when you meet him.

Though he likely would have done so anyway, the last instruction confuses Jackson.

Why should I wear a hood?

Conjure a Reflection scroll, and you will see.

With a snap, Jackson conjures the proper scroll and unfolds it to gaze upon the reflective surface. The mirror shows him a face he hardly recognizes. The skin has an unnatural gray cast to it and wrinkles at several places across his forehead. Uncomfortable with the changes, he sends the scroll away and looks down at his hands. They too have a gray cast to them that reminds him of Marina's damaged hand.

Can it be reversed?

Perhaps in time, but for now, you will have to wear an illusion when meeting people who know you. However, I believe it may be good for the Supreme Huntmaster to see what he's truly dealing with. Speak with his daughter, Dina, as well. I have molded her heart for years. It is time she officially joins us.

What of Lady Christa?

She is of no immediate consequence. Leave her alone unless she interferes.

Relieved, Jackson conjures a scroll from his collection of undead, moves to a random place in the forest, and releases them. He repeats the process a dozen more times, forming a wide circle around the cabin containing his niece and her friends. Part of him wishes to witness the coming battle, but due to Daniel's Seeker abilities, Jackson cannot risk going near a structure that may register his presence unless he wants to hide under a privacy spell.

I will share their progress with you.

Chapter 22:
Guild Contract

Home of Daniel and Vic, Karnok Mountains
Two days earlier (Twelve years and four months after Marina's death)
(Vic is thirteen years old)

There's enough food and water to last until tomorrow. The blocks to brace the doors are where they should be. The weapons are accessible but out of the way. The stockpile of firewood is good. The roof hasn't leaked in a while. The back fence still has a hole, and I didn't repair the wards. Katrina should be able to defend the garden from wildlife. Anything else can wait for my return. Now to deal with Vic.

Daniel has delayed the coming conversation the entire morning and much of the afternoon, but Katrina's arrival removes his last excuse for leaving. Closing the cabin door softly to avoid waking the exhausted Shapeshifter, Daniel finds his daughter in the vegetable garden attacking weeds. He doesn't need to see her deep frown to know she's upset. The large pile of weeds sitting next to her gives him a clue. Force of habit makes him scan their surroundings. Nothing seems out of the ordinary, but that could change instantly.

The sun has moved to an angle that causes the towering trees to cast long shadows across much of the garden, but Vic's currently sitting in a patch of sunlight.

A lump forms in Daniel's throat as he watches his daughter grip another weed, yank it clear, and toss it onto the pile. The pale blue, short-sleeved dress suits her perfectly. The section lining her collar and forming the sleeve cuffs feature white lace and a series of fabric beads that render additional jewelry unnecessary. Two thick braids hanging down past her shoulders contain her golden hair. The sadness etched into her expression enhances her beauty and pierces Daniel's heart.

She's growing up.

The thought stirs up mixed emotions. The joy of seeing her blossom into a young woman gets tempered by the ever-present fear that he won't always be able to protect her. He wants to forget leaving, sit down beside Vic, and help her weed the garden like they have so many times before.

"Why are you leaving this time?" asks Vic.

"I have to go to Bastion to see the Supreme Huntmaster and get permission to take a Guild contract," says Daniel. The *this time* part of her comment is slightly unfair, but he doesn't argue the point. He has only taken a handful of solo trips away from the cabin in the last year and only two of them went beyond three days.

Forgetting the weeds, Vic fixes her eyes on him.

"Why can't I come with you? I can help, and I won't get in the way."

"Katrina's already here," says Daniel. "She's napping inside to recover from the journey. Tellen should arrive soon as well. Who would keep them company if we both left?"

"They could come with us," says Vic. Her voice carries hints of her rising desperation. "If you don't want us to go to Bastion, that's fine. But tell us where you'll be, and we can meet you there."

Eventually, Daniel will travel to the city of Urdik, one of the last places on Aeris he'd ever take his daughter. Councilman Jelan Balewa and his wife sought Guild help to find their kidnapped son because the city authorities hold deep biases against anybody who opposes their extreme views. Fearing the thought of danger might make the prospect more appealing, Daniel stays silent on the issue of Urdik being a terrible place for anybody with Saroth connections. There will be time enough later for Vic to discover the many things wrong with the world. If he can preserve her peace of mind another few days, he'll do it.

The Resolute practically run Urdik.

"I can stay with the people you're trying to help like I did in Coldhaven last year," Vic presses. "You said they were happy to have me to comfort them. Why is this different?"

Because the people of Coldhaven wouldn't sell you to Resolute thugs because your mother happened to be Saroth.

"Because I need to be free to teleport anywhere, anytime," says Daniel. Seeing the words hit Vic hard, he rushes forward and kneels. "It's not about being in the way, Vic. It's about letting me do my job quickly, so I can come home to you. Can I have a hug?"

Turning her face away from him, Vic tries to hide her tears.

Daniel considers telling her what little he knows about the job. She might be happier knowing he intends to save a young boy from kidnappers. The moment passes, and he says nothing since he's never been one to share contract details with anybody, especially not before he has every fact.

Vic sniffles and her face reddens.

Holding in a sigh, Daniel tries to mask his disappointment. When his knee starts to stiffen, he climbs to his feet.

"Stay with Katrina and Tellen," he instructs. "If anything goes wrong, go to Coldhaven and speak with the village elder. There's enough water to last the day and food for two to three days, but if you need to hunt, Tellen or Katrina should know where to find good game."

"I know how to track animals," Vic mutters. "*You* showed me how to hunt."

A few lessons can't match years of hunting classes and even that can't match the animal instincts of a Shapeshifter in the right form. Katrina's ability to become a beetle, a snake, or a dog makes her the perfect scout.

"I know." Daniel holds up a hand to ward off Vic's scorn. "But they both have more experience than you do. Marcus said Katrina was in the middle of a month-long training exercise with her master when I called, and Tellen just finished a long hunt to help the Kesh villagers improve their food supply."

A twinge of guilt smacks Daniel. After the long mission, Tellen had planned to go to Cardeth to visit his family. He had been halfway there by the time Daniel's request caught up to him.

"Why did you invite them both?" asks Vic. "They don't even like each other."

The statement hurts, but Daniel doesn't have time to correct her misconception. Tellen and Katrina come from different worlds and possess fierce loyalty to their people, but their friendship with Vic proves they're more open-minded than most of their peers.

"That's not true," Daniel protests, scrambling for a better argument. He doesn't want to delve into the full answer. He'd initially invited Tellen because he trusts the Guardian to protect Vic. Katrina's invite came when further thought told Daniel his daughter shouldn't be alone with a seventeen-year-old young man, especially now that she's becoming a young woman. Placing his hands on Vic's shoulders, Daniel squeezes gently. "They hardly know each other, and they've spent a long time learning only about their own people. Maybe this time together will change that. What matters is they both love you and will protect you."

"I'll need protection from boredom," Vic grumbles.

"I hope so." Daniel pulls her into a brief hug, grateful when she returns it. "I love you."

"I love you, too, but I'm still mad at you."

Chuckling, Daniel kisses the top of her head.

"I'll accept that if it keeps you safe." He pulls back and waves toward the cabin. "Better go in. I know you hate watching me teleport."

"I hate watching you leave," Vic clarifies. "It doesn't matter how it happens."

Daniel's stunned by her answer. She throws her arms around him and squeezes tightly before releasing him and turning away quickly, running for the cabin.

I'm sorry, Vic. If I could stay with you always, I would, but there's evil in this world. I have to do my part to fight it.

Before he can find or invent a reason to stay, Daniel teleports to Bastion.

After hearing his request, one of the portal guards escorts Daniel to Jordan's office.

Several minutes elapse. Daniel concentrates on not pacing.

Over the next hour, three others arrive and enter the office. Daniel didn't think Jordan the type for such pettiness, but he understands the point: non-active members are low priority to the very busy Supreme Huntmaster.

The delay gives Daniel a chance to think about his daughter. Vic still hasn't shown much more magic, though there have been a few more instances where her whole body lights up. Having her resemble Marina in more than looks pleases him. He's proud she enjoys helping people, even if she doesn't get many chances to do so.

She'll do a lot of good if she accepts the inheritance.

Even as the thought forms, Daniel knows Vic has too much of him to be content spending her life in house council and regional manager meetings. The notion sparks another question.

What would other children have been like?

The mental image of a dark-haired little boy with his features forms before Daniel forces his thoughts elsewhere.

I have one daughter. Vic's all I need. Is she your Chosen Redeemer?

Daniel hopes for an answer from the Lady of Light, but he's not surprised when he hears nothing. She has spoken with him in the past, but the Ancient Ones do not answer to mortal beings.

Some signs say so.

Vic is a child of both magic races. She also wears the magic bracers, even though they technically belong to Daniel. According to the prophecy, the Lady's Chosen Redeemer will send the Outcast's army back into the Darklands and destroy the link between the natural and spiritual world.

What does that mean?

Interpretations run the gamut from literal to purely metaphorical.

Before Daniel can wrestle the ideas too long, one of the Pirok Guards calls him over and waves him into the Supreme Huntmaster's office.

"Sorry for the wait," says Jordan. "It's been harder to manage schedules without Mason."

"What happened to him?" Daniel asks, trying to recall the name.

"He left."

Although Jordan doesn't elaborate, Daniel's Seeker Gift skims one other piece of information. Huntmaster Mason Pine moved to Urdik to train the Homeguard.

I thought Galeric trained the Homeguard.

Dropping the point, Daniel skips to his main purpose in coming.

"I want to move to active status and take the contract from Jelan Balewa."

"How did you hear about that?" Jordan demands.

"The councilman sought a Minder to reach Marcus Polani. He relayed the message to me," Daniel explains.

"Why you?" Jordan presses.

"My parents died in Urdik," says Daniel. "Master Balewa's family looked after me until the Guild could get the bodies moved to Aridel for the funeral. I guess he remembered I'm a Seeker."

"Your timing is excellent," Jordan comments, reaching into the Veil to draw out the contract. "We were just informed of the job yesterday. It's quite lucrative. I've sent messengers after some other Seekers, but I'm not sure any can drop their contracts quickly enough to make a difference. I was going to send some Guardians who have handled similar contracts."

"I can start right away," says Daniel.

Jordan shakes his head.

"This isn't the real contract. It's just a copy with the details,"

Jordan explains, offering Daniel the scroll. "You'll have to meet the councilman and his wife in Temperance the day after tomorrow to sign the official scroll. This one's not even enchanted."

Taking the scroll, Daniel reads the description. He learns several things: the boy's name is Lekan Balewa, he's six and a half years old, and the meeting place is not at the councilman's estate.

"You can take that with you," says Jordan.

"Why is the meeting in Temperance and not Urdik?" Daniel wonders, "and why is there a delay?"

"There's unrest in Urdik." Jordan pulls another contract from the Veil, picks up a quill sitting in an inkwell, and signs the bottom with big, bold letters. "I can't say why they set the meeting up for when they did, but I gather it will be safer not to be seen together. You should also avoid the traveler's portals in Urdik, but the one from here to Temperance should be safe enough. You can spend the extra time here in Bastion or in one of the Temperance properties."

He offers Daniel the scroll and the quill, so he can sign the contract that will move him back to active Guild status.

"Welcome back. When you finish with this contract, I have a few more that could use your attention."

"Thank you." As soon as Daniel finishes signing, a coin appears. Satisfaction and excitement fill him as he picks up the coin and tucks it into the Veil.

Turning to leave, Daniel's Seeker senses pick up on a dark presence he hasn't felt in years. He halts mid-step and regards Jordan curiously. A sweep of Jordan's desk contents reveals a crumpled scrap of parchment.

"What's wrong?" Jordan asks. He meets Daniel's gaze then follows his line of vision to the scrap. "That's nothing." The words have too much force to be believed.

"It's from Jackson Castaloni," Daniel murmurs.

"As I said, it's nothing," Jordan insists, waving dismissively. "He wants to meet. Given my schedule, that could take months to arrange."

"Be careful," Daniel warns. "He's dangerous. He tried to kill Marina once."

Probably more than once.

He raises a hand before Jordan can ask any probing questions.

"I can't give you details about that, but I assure you it has nothing to do with the Guild."

Daniel leaves before Jordan decides to question him further. He doesn't think sharing the details can hurt anybody at this point, but he intends to honor the promise to never reveal what truly happened at River's Edge. He doesn't know if the Saroth laws have changed in the two decades since those events, but with Marina and Gabriel both gone, Daniel sees no reason to dredge up the matter.

Chapter 23:
Undead Encounter

Home of Daniel and Vic, Karnok Mountains
Two days earlier (Twelve years and four months after Marina's death)
(Vic is thirteen years old)

Despite racing for the back door, Vic stops running as soon as she knows her father's gone. Dashing away two tears, she spins around and peers at the empty patch of ground where he last stood.

Stop it! He'll be back. You can't spend your whole life waiting for him to return.

"What else can I do?" Vic whispers the question aloud, not quite ready to accept being alone. She considers waking Katrina but rejects the idea because she knows the journey up the mountain can be exhausting.

Even for a Shapeshifter.

The thought of Katrina's abilities sends jealousy sailing through Vic, but she pushes it away. Shapeshifting would be fun, but she can't think of many practical uses for the Gift. It would be great for escaping but not fighting. If she had Destroyer Gifts like her mother or Guardian Gifts like Tellen, she would be able to fight well. Vic doesn't even know why that's important to her.

It's not like anybody's going to trek deep into the Karnok Mountains to attack you.

As her attention lands on the pile of weeds, Vic considers dealing with it. Her father hadn't ordered her to stay in the cabin, but he would disapprove of her venturing off without Katrina.

She's tired. It's only weeds. I won't even leave the fenced-in area.

Over the years, the portion of yard protected by a fence grew as

Father cut down trees for wood and building projects. From the cabin's back door to the fence nearest the line of trees was probably only forty paces. Dumping the weeds in the side yards to the left or right would be easier, but they always used the back for brush they didn't want the wind blowing back into the garden.

Standing over the pile of weeds, Vic considers her options. Carrying the brush with her hands and arms would take several trips. Retrieving a basket from inside would make the job doable in two or three trips. Using her dress might allow her to accomplish it in one trip.

Even with the prospect of weed disposal being the highlight of her afternoon, Vic chooses the one-trip option. Sitting on the ground, she scoops up the weeds and bundles them into the bottom portion of her dress. Without the gloves she wears whenever she's not home, the contrast between her two hands is stark. The left hand has perfectly healthy skin, while the right one looks gray and lifeless. Dirt covers both hands as she moves the pile of weeds into place and rises. She might have to change into something cleaner, depending on how much dirt clings to the dress, but maybe that will give her a good excuse to convince Katrina to visit the nearby stream with her. Excited by the prospect, Vic hurries to dump the weeds.

"Hello, Vic," says a cheerful male voice.

Startled, Vic yelps and drops her bundle of skirt and weeds. Recovering quickly, she glares at the speaker as he emerges from the woods. He's taller than she remembers. Jogging forward, Tellen plants his hands on the fence railing and hauls his body up and over the obstacle with a huntsman's easy grace.

A crack sounds, and the fence section collapses, tossing Tellen toward Vic. He rolls easily to his feet and shakes dirt from his blond hair.

"That was unexpected," he comments, sweeping his gaze over the broken rail. "Does your father keep spare rails around?"

"I don't know. Maybe by the woodpile out front," says Vic.

"I think we have a bigger problem," says Katrina, appearing next to the fallen rail. She picks up one of the pieces and changes its angle so they can see it.

Vic barely has time to see the piece of wood, before Tellen grabs her shoulders and turns her around, but she notices that half the rail shows a clean cut while the rest is jagged.

"What does that mean?" Vic asks, digging her heels into the soft ground to resist being moved.

"You should return to the cabin," says Katrina. "I'll check the rest of the fence and join you shortly." With that, she takes her beetle form and zips toward the fence then scuttles along the top edge before disappearing on the far side.

Tellen nudges Vic.

"You heard the Saroth," he says. "Move. It's not safe out here."

"What are you talking about?" Vic wonders. "We're on a mountain in the middle a forest very far from the nearest village."

"We're isolated and exposed," Tellen counters. "We'll be safer back by the cabin. Don't make me carry you."

"Do it," Vic challenges, crossing her arms.

Tellen scoops her up and starts jogging.

A surprised scream morphs into laughter as Vic finds herself staring at the ground, having been tossed over Tellen's right shoulder.

"Put me down!" she orders.

He does so before making a twirling motion with his hand and pointing at the cabin.

"Help me dump the weeds first," she says.

"They can wait," Tellen assures her, not budging.

Grunting, Vic reluctantly turns and trudges to the cabin. The back door leads to the common room. The right side as one enters from the back has a couch, some wooden chairs, a low table, and the neat stacks of books and scrolls. The opposite side contains the kitchen table, the stove, and storage space for food and water.

They wait tensely until Katrina returns and reports.

"Almost every rail has been damaged."

The speculation over who, how, and why somebody would bother goes nowhere. Eventually, Tellen convinces them it's late enough that they should go to sleep.

The next day passes in a boring blur. Vic tries everything from weeding to reading to sparring with Tellen to guessing which creature Katrina will form next or which weapon Tellen will pull from the Veil. She tries to convince them to let her go hunting, but when the time comes, they host a brief debate before agreeing to a contest to see who can find game first while staying within sight of the cabin. Katrina eventually wins because she can range farther faster than Tellen. She returns triumphantly with two large rabbits. Having lost the contest, Tellen cleans the kills and turns part of it into their evening meal.

The second day starts much the same as the first, but by early afternoon, Vic runs out of garden to weed.

"Let's play darts," says Tellen.

Vic doesn't want to play, and Katrina voices no opinion on the matter.

"It will pass the time," Tellen argues. "Come on, three rounds. We don't even need to put up stakes."

"Fine, but you have to set up the board," says Vic. She points to the corner where they store the game. Normally, darts is an outdoor game, but the cabin walls bear witness to the many times Father has not enforced that rule.

Katrina's three throws land on the board, but it's clear she only plays so Vic will. Tellen's three strikes land in the center because it's not really a challenge for him at this distance. Vic goes last. Her first throw lodges in the wall above the board. The second and third darts pierce the couch in two different places.

"I win," Tellen announces.

Before she can respond, Vic's vision clouds. A tingling sensation crawls through her stomach. Light starts leaking out of her mouth.

Not again!

***

The instant Vic's body glows, the Arkonai boy whips his two main daggers off his belt and moves closer to her. Katrina takes her dog form and growls.

"Vic, wait!" Tellen shouts.

Still shining, Vic sprints past them and runs into the back yard.

Katrina follows close behind, rushing into the clear space.

Loud cracking noises sound up and down the fence. Turning into a beetle, Katrina flies straight up and spins to view the entire scene.

Screams ring out.

Armed figures crash through the fence from every side, brandishing many kinds of weapons. Their clothes hang awkwardly on their bodies. Empty sockets stare sightlessly at Vic. Fading sunlight bathes those to Katrina's left. Shadows fall upon those to her right. Three approaching from the back fire arrows at Vic, but Tellen knocks her to the ground and the arrows fly past them into the door.

Undead.

Every story Katrina has heard failed to convey the hopelessness and terror that grips her as their cries grow more frantic.

Vic bounces back to her feet even faster than Tellen.

A zombie launches a spear at Vic.

Shrieking, she leaps and catches the spear.

Light flashes.

An explosion knocks Katrina's beetle form end over end. She loses count of the number of times she flips before halting the involuntary flight. Orienting quickly, she dives down, aiming for the nearest cluster of zombies.

The flight time lets her see Tellen fight three attackers at once. He plunges both daggers into the one on his right, yanks them clear, and buries them into the next one before kicking a third. The first two burst into dust.

Not sure how to help, Katrina moves over the nearest zombie, flips to dog form, and allows the bulky body to carry her down onto the creature's shoulders.

A sword swings down at her.

She has no time to dodge, so she flips to beetle form and lets the blade pass. As the sword slams into the zombie she knocked off balance, Katrina zips toward the new attacker. Drawing near the creature's neck, she transforms into a snake and wraps her new body around the target. She's back in beetle form as a third zombie removes the head of the second while aiming for her.

Dust coats her.

Taking dog form, Katrina lands on the ground and bites down hard on the third zombie's leg, shaking her head back and forth rapidly to increase the damage. The creature bursts apart. A glance up shows Katrina a shiny dagger before it flies back into Tellen's hand. Choosing to be a beetle again, she flies up to check the battle's progress.

Most zombies swarm around Vic who wields the spear like a staff. After thrusting the pointed end through one creature's chest, Vic pulls back, grips the weapon with both hands, spins right, and rakes the blade through two more. The weapon passes through the bodies like they're smoke, turning them to dust before Katrina's eyes.

Tellen sees none of this. He's busy entertaining two more zombies. Unlike the others, bright blue light burns in the eye sockets of this pair. The creatures take turns testing his defenses, striking with excellent coordination so the Arkonai huntsman gets no time to rest between parries. Blue sparks travel up and down the enemy swords.

Tellen cries out in pain as the next sword strike lands against his daggers, but he manages to hold the blades and send lightning out and into the two zombies.

They stagger back.

Dropping to the ground, Katrina chooses dog form and charges the nearest zombie, aiming to knock into the creature's legs.

She clips one, knocking it further off balance. By the time she turns to renew the attack, Vic's spear is threaded through both creatures. Tellen finishes them with a long blast of lightning.

With terrible shrieks, the pair turns to dust.

The spear hangs in midair.

The tip detaches.

Vic kneels as if to pray. Her bracers gleam and cover her forearms and part of her hands.

The spear top darts away almost too quickly to track.

Katrina reverts to human form as the blade hurls itself back and forth across the yard.

More frustrated screams and shouts arise.

Bodies thud to the ground before breaking down into miniature dust clouds.

The wind picks up, sweeping the mountain clear of zombie dust.

The spear tip returns to Vic and flops to the ground next to her.

She looks around in a daze, closes her eyes, and curls onto her side, narrowly missing the spear tip.

Alarmed, Katrina rushes over and drops down beside Vic. Her head comes uncomfortably close to the Arkonai boy as he too leans down to check on their friend.

"Get some water," Tellen orders.

Despite the reluctance to obey commands barked by an Arkonai, Katrina takes dog form and races for the cabin. Somehow, the battle had roiled well away from the door. She tries to concentrate on the task but can't help replaying the fight in her mind. She's been training as a Shapeshifter and sparring with many different combat instructors for years. She's seen many strange things in the Enchanted Forest and elsewhere on missions with Master Talini. Nothing experienced in her sixteen years of life has come close to this.

What kind of magic was that?

Katrina arrives at the cabin before getting to consider the question. She becomes human, slips into the cabin, and fills a cup with water from one of the buckets in the kitchen. Rarely has she wished for different Gifts, but as she struggles not to spill the water, Katrina longs for Conjurer Gifts. She steadies herself by thinking over her training. She doesn't have a cat form, but her master often referred to having the grace of a cat in any body.

To facilitate slow, steady walking, Katrina again considers the fight and Vic's magic.

Tellen's ability to produce lightning proves that not every set of powers belongs to a single school of magic. On some camping trips, Vic's father told them stories. He'd said Marina—Vic's mother—had trained to heal people despite having Destroyer Gifts.

That must be what prompted rumors of her being a witch.

The irritation at how stupid and cruel people can be causes Katrina to spill some of the water, but she reaches Tellen and Vic with about half a cup to offer. Relief sweeps through her when she sees Vic sitting up. Lacking something profound to say, Katrina holds out the cup of water.

"What are you doing here?" Vic asks, receiving the cup with a polite nod of thanks. "Where's my father?"

Katrina exchanges a worried glance with the Arkonai boy.

"Your father's on a hunt, Vic," says Tellen.

"He wanted us to stay with you because he doesn't know when he'll be back," Katrina explains.

"How long has my father been gone? Where'd this spear come from?" Vic gingerly picks up the sharp blade.

"Do you remember anything about the fight?" asks Tellen.

"What fight?" Vic swivels her head from Tellen to Katrina.

"Guess that gives us our answer," says Katrina, not bothering to answer Vic's question about the length of her father's absence. They don't have time to wonder how much of her memory has gone blank. "Can you get up? We should go inside."

"We should leave," says Tellen. "There's no telling when more of those things will come."

Katrina considers arguing, but she's terrified his prediction will come true.

"What things?" asks Vic.

"Undead people," Katrina answers.

Together, they get Vic up to her feet and guide her inside the cabin.

"Grab a few blankets," Tellen instructs. "I'll pack the food."

"Where are we going?" asks Vic.

"We'll follow your father's emergency plan," Tellen answers. "It's late to start traveling tonight, but that can't be helped. The cabin's not safe. We'll head to the nearest village. That means we go to Coldhaven."

Chapter 24:
Final Preparations

Home of Daniel and Vic, Karnok Mountains
Same day as the zombie attack (Twelve years and four months after Marina's death)
(Vic is thirteen years old)

Jackson studies the ground carefully, finding weapons but few other signs of the undead force sent to dispose of his niece. As he finds swords, spears, arrows, bows, and other debris from the battle, Jackson conjures them back into his armory at Fort Medron. Alec can clean them later.

Looks like I'm meeting the Supreme Huntmaster tomorrow.

Victoria lives, but she is vulnerable. Find something that belongs to her and summon the Denkari. My spirit warriors should be able to track her as well as any Minder. Remember to take precautions against Daniel's Gifts. He is distracted now, but he may yet meddle.

Summoning a privacy scroll, Jackson releases the spell over his body. The effect won't last as long as it would if cast over a room, but it should contain his presence for the time he intends to spend in the cabin.

What kind of object will I need?

Size matters less than sentiment, but you will have to burn this object completely. A bigger item will require a greater energy commitment from you, but the supply of slaves must be renewed before the summoning ceremony anyway. Having to retrieve one or two extra should not matter. The disappearances will not be the main concern of anybody for long.

150

Stepping into the cabin, Jackson peers around before starting his search. The main room consists of a common area and a kitchen. The common area doesn't hold much of interest. A dart board has been mounted above the couch. They must have been interrupted mid-game because darts still stick out of the wall and couch.

Past the kitchen, there's a hallway leading to the bedrooms. After the second bedroom, Jackson finds a small storage room. The hallway ends in another door. This one leads out to a well-worn path to an outhouse. Jackson had forgotten some Arkonai dwellings have such primitive things. Most of Saroth society has long since answered the problem of waste with magical solutions.

Retracing his steps to Victoria's room, Jackson scans for a small object for his ritual. The bed holds some sheets but no blankets. The end table by the bed contains an empty cup and a scroll. A few wooden crates hold various items of clothing.

Doesn't she own any jewelry?

I am seeing what you see. Take one of her shirts and go. It will suffice.

Plucking a green shirt off the pile in the closest crate, Jackson tucks the item into his robes and conjures himself to his study in Fort Medron.

Footsteps thunder down the stairs.

How does he always know when I'm home?

Alec is a Minder.

The announcement alarms Jackson.

Can he read my thoughts?

Not yet. His skills are powerful but untrained and undirected. For now, the Gift manifests mostly as visions and dreams. He can probably sense your mind, even if he cannot yet reach out and communicate directly. Perhaps it's time to have your mother seek a proper tutor for the boy.

Jackson makes a noncommittal noise. He enjoys having the boy as his apprentice. There's a refreshing curiosity and innocence about Alec.

"Uncle Jack! You're back!" Alec races in and throws his arms around Jackson's waist. The boy grunts and moves back a step. "You're softer."

Jackson removes Victoria's shirt from inside his robes.

"What's that?" Alec asks.

"It's a shirt that belongs to your cousin Victoria," says Jackson.

"I know Vic," says Alec. "Lady Fia told me about her. She said Vic's mother was sister to you and Papa." Alec tilts his head. "Why do you have her shirt?"

Be cautious about what you tell him. He will want to protect her.

"Because we need to find her," Jackson explains. "She's in trouble."

"Could a Minder find her?" Alec wonders.

"Yes, but that might take too long," says Jackson. "A Minder who has met her would have to locate her and then send somebody else to help. I'm going to summon servants that can track her. Would you like to help?"

Alec brightens and nods vigorously.

Jackson hands him the shirt and has him fold it very carefully before delivering it to the fireplace. Upon realizing they must destroy the shirt, Alec protests, but he quiets down when reminded that the ritual could save Victoria's life.

They share a simple evening meal Jackson conjures from the food set aside for him in the main Castaloni estate in Jorash. He thought his mother might have the cook discontinue the tradition of always having food on hand for him once he bought his own estate in the city, but she did not. Since her cook knows his preferences better than his own, he still takes advantage of the boon.

Alec pleads to stay up and watch the ritual, but Jackson sends him to do evening chores before bed. The arena chains need to be checked and cleaned. The sand needs to be raked. The walls have no significant bloodstains to clean, but the holding pens must have fresh straw.

Jackson considers using a sleep spell on Alec before fetching the new batch of prisoners. His energy reserves would be enough to complete the first ritual, which will establish Victoria as the target, but he doesn't mind putting it off a few hours. Sitting alone in his study, Jackson tries to pass the time by reviewing the words to the more complicated summoning spell. Questions distract him.

What should I do if Victoria survives the Denkari attack?

Have her taken to Fort Amareth. It has a dormant Darkland Portal. Seize the bracers or make her open a stable portal.

Should I continue with the Arkonai plan for tracking her? What happens if the huntsmen and the Denkari get in each other's way?

Once the Denkari have a target, they will not rest until they

152

destroy her, but they can suffer temporary defeats. The Arkonai plan is still a good one, and if our help should meet each other, we will see who is stronger.

Jackson wants to believe their plans cannot fail, but he's seen too many brilliant schemes collapse for stupid reasons. Last year, he'd led the Arkonai boy called Tellen right to a baydonberry patch. Thinking they were blueberries, the young man had successfully poisoned Victoria and the Polani girl, but because the girl was fifteen at the time, a team of bodyguards appeared before the hired hands could finish the job.

Katrina has outgrown that protection. Her skills as a Shapeshifter are admirable, but she should not be a real threat to the huntsmen. Her forms are better for scouting and evading.

What about Tellen? He must be competent if Daniel trusts him with Victoria's care.

He is a good fighter, but he is a Guardian. Tellen should not have the ability to teleport at will. Separate them from Victoria as quickly as possible.

How go the plans for a war? Should I be concerned?

The Arkonai Brotherhood has faded to almost nothing, and the Resolute are stronger than ever. The Supreme Huntmaster and the Council are almost where I want them. Their fear of the Darkland creatures should push them to a holy war soon, but they may need more evidence of Saroth involvement.

Jackson understands that to mean he may have to betray some of those who have helped him maintain Darkland portals in the Ashlands and the Badlands.

A task for another time. Go collect your slaves.

Will Alec be all right alone?

I will monitor the boy.

Jackson feels foolish for worrying about Alec. The boy has spent countless hours alone in Fort Medron and never come to harm. Pride sweeps the discomfort away. In a matter of days or weeks, Jackson should be able to summon the Master's spirit from the Darklands.

You'll be free to work without a host.

Soon, my servant, but you must first call forth the Denkari. Their presence will be part of my anchor.

After checking to make sure his hunting scrolls can be reached easily, Jackson moves through the Veil to Temperance.

The guard tenses at his sudden appearance in the dark alley.

Before the man can speak, Jackson tosses a Transportation scroll at his feet. Startled screams come from the guard, the prisoners, and several other voices. Jackson returns to Fort Medron to see what he's caught. He's pleased to have attracted extra bodies tonight. It will save him from a second trip. Similar traps have been used successfully against those buying prisoners as slaves. Jackson would have perished in such traps many times over if he didn't have his master's blessing and abilities to break free.

The spell dumps everybody into the arena's sandy pit. Since he specifically set it to release them well above the ground, the bodies make significant thudding noises as they strike the sand.

Jackson appears at the top of the stairs.

The guard and the three prisoners are expected guests. The four additional guards are a bonus. They must have been under a concealment spell. Surprisingly, nobody perished in the transition.

The three prisoners chatter.

"Where are we?" inquires one prisoner, still sitting in the sand.

"You said we'd be free if we do this," says a second prisoner, glaring at the first guard.

"I demand release!" cries the third, shaking his chained hands at the four unexpected guards.

Jackson ignores the prisoners. His master hasn't joined his spirit today, but his presence in the room heightens Jackson's magical senses. Unfortunately, all the new guards are Bereft. The guard he had been communicating with to make the arrangements has minor Healing Gifts. One prisoner has Conjuring Gifts while the other two have Destroyer Gifts. The prisoner with the right skill conjures a sword to hand and angles it to ward off the guards. The Destroyers do nothing.

What's wrong with them? Why aren't they creating lighting to fend off the guards?

Those with Destroyer Gifts were never trained to use their power. This is common for Saroth raised in a neutral city. The poor do not always prioritize magic education. Do you wish to fight them?

Not today. The four Bereft won't do me much good, especially if they're exhausted from fighting. I may have to use the guard with Healing gifts for the first ritual.

Very well. Move those you wish to keep in reserve to the wall chains. Leave the rest in the center. I will shield the walls while you work so as not to disturb them until their turn.

The men stare at each other uneasily. The Bereft guards sway and stagger like drunk men. Jackson conjures the swords and daggers away from the guards, afraid they might kill each other before collapsing. The first prisoner, who has yet to rise, lies back in the sand. The other two look at him then sink to their knees beside him. Both pitch forward and land on their faces. Soon, eight sleeping bodies decorate the sand.

Knowing the work ahead will be long, hot, and dirty, Jackson stops by his Jorash estate to instruct servants to prepare a warm bath for him.

Wishing Alec was old enough to help with the grunt work, Jackson hauls the prisoners to the arena walls and chains them in place. He uses their original chains to link the four Bereft guards together. For the Healer, he conjures a scroll containing enchanted rope and applies it in four sections, binding the man's ankles, legs, hands, and arms. To further hinder his captives' movements, Jackson conjures a heavy tree trunk and chains each prisoner to a portion of it.

At the snap of his fingers, a metal firepit forms between Jackson and his prisoners. Finally, he calls the green shirt he'd left up in his study. Setting the shirt in the firepit, Jackson voices the incantation. Letting his body be a conduit for the magic, he lets life energy flow into the sand at his feet and draws more from the prisoners. As he reaches the last line, Jackson uses the Saroth gift for fire to reduce the cloth to ashes.

Needing to clear the space, Jackson sends the tree trunk and bodies to Malcorius's cave on Mount Casilisk in the Desolate Mountains. If the black dragon has no need for the additional food, he will let his followers enjoy the feast.

After gathering the ashes into a leather pouch, Jackson moves the firepit back into the storage room. Next, he spreads the ashes in a thin line, creating a wide circle at the arena's center.

Weary but satisfied, Jackson steps through the Veil to his Jorash estate for a cleansing bath.

Everything is ready, Master.

Chapter 25:
Thought Transfer

Lady Mekrian's House of Discreet Transactions, City of Temperance
Same day as the zombie attack (Twelve years and four months after Marina's death)
(Vic is thirteen years old)

At the appointed time, an attendant ushers Daniel to a small room in the wing opposite where the meeting with Lady Corabelle took place. Nodding thanks, Daniel enters and shuts the door before observing the surroundings. Like every other business room, this one contains no windows. The furniture lacks the ornate designs and fancy upholstery found in the other wing, but the general layout has not changed. A round table holds three seats instead of two, and a couch stretches along the back wall. A teapot and three cups take up the center of the table.

A distinguished, dark-skinned couple rises from the couch as Daniel enters. Despite not having seen the man for close to thirty years, he recognizes Jelan Balewa immediately. This version wears a red suit with a long tunic and has no hair instead of the thick black hair the councilman had possessed as a young man. Several rings line each of his fingers. Daniel remembers each one signifies a key event in Jelan's life, but he cannot remember which occasion each ring signifies. The last they'd seen each other, Jelan had only worn two rings, one for joining the Merchant Guild and one for being betrothed.

Jelan speeds through the introductions.

Daniel has never met the woman, so he accepts her proffered right hand in both of his and bows deeply. Many thick gold bracelets clink as Akuna Balewa clasps his hands briefly. She wears a gray dress with an intricate red and gold swirling pattern that covers her right shoulder while leaving the left bare.

As a Seeker, Daniel has met quite a few parents of missing children. Jelan and Akuna appear calmer than most, but their anger and worry are apparent in every movement and surface thought.

"Thank you for coming, Seeker Daniel," says Jelan in his deep voice. The Bereft accent gives the words a flowing, musical quality. He waves at the chair closest to Daniel and pulls one of the remaining chairs out for Akuna before sitting in the one to his wife's left. "I'm sorry we could not host you in our home."

"We are watched by the Homeguard," Akuna explains. "They say it is for our protection, but it is only to know if we obey the commands of those who took Lekan."

"How long has your son been gone?" Daniel asks.

"They took him three days ago in the morning while we were walking back from the market," Akuna answers. "One moment I held his hand. The next, I awoke holding only a scroll."

"Do you have the scroll?" Daniel wonders. If he can touch something held by the kidnappers, he might be able to trace them through the city streets.

"It burnt to ashes as soon as I read it," Akuna says shaking her head, "but the message was enchanted so I would remember."

"What did it say?" Daniel prompts.

"I am to vote in favor of the Safe City Laws being put to the People's Council in three days," says Jelan. "We are promised Lekan's return once the measures pass."

"Do you believe they'll keep their word?" asks Daniel.

"Aye. We do. This is rare but not unheard of in Urdik politics," Akuna reports.

That explains them being comfortable with a delay.

"Why did you ask for me?" Daniel suspects the answer but seeks confirmation. "What is included in the proposed laws?"

"I cannot support them," Jelan declares. "They are thinly disguised efforts to legalize Resolute beliefs that our problems stem from the Saroth."

"They want to force Saroth to pay additional taxes to answer for wrongs recorded centuries ago," Akuna explains. "That is only one example. They also wish to have them register with the Homeguard and move to one section within the city. There is more but it does not matter now."

"They are wrong, and I have made clear my stance on them," says Jelan, "but I cannot vote with my heart if it costs my son's life."

"You won't have to," Daniel assures him. Although working with a deadline is not ideal, he draws hope from the fact that the kidnappers will strive to keep the boy alive until the vote. "I will take the contract. Did you bring anything that belongs to your son? It can help with Seeking him."

Akuna draws a tiny ring out of her left pocket and reluctantly hands it to Daniel.

"This was his first ring. He has outgrown it, but we have not had a chance to get him another."

"I don't need to keep it," Daniel says. "I just need to hold it for a few seconds." He closes his fist around the ring and focuses his Gifts on memorizing the feel of the ring's owner. Once finished, he hands the ring back.

Looking relieved, Akuna eagerly accepts the gold band.

The councilman hands Daniel the official contract along with more thanks.

The details recount almost everything discussed, but the amount surprises Daniel. It's much higher than normal Guild rates for jobs of a similar nature, even accounting for the fact that he hasn't taken contracts in years. He frowns but doesn't bring up the matter now. The councilman and his wife would know nothing of the rates anyway. They would have merely asked for help and been quoted a price.

Why is it so high?

"I will start my search tonight," Daniel promises. Turning to Akuna, he adds an important question. "Do you remember the exact location where the kidnapping occurred?"

"Of course, I will show you," says Akuna.

"No!" The protest comes from Daniel and Jelan simultaneously.

"It is too dangerous for you to be on the streets," says Jelan.

"I accept the danger to myself." Akuna sets her jaw and inclines her head.

"It's also dangerous for us to be seen together," Daniel explains. "We cannot let anybody know you've sought a Seeker. That would endanger Lekan." He holds up a hand like he might have to physically stop her from marching back to Urdik.

"There may be another way if you are willing to work with a Minder."

"Could a Minder find our son?" Jelan asks. His dark eyes shine with hope.

"Probably not, unless the Minder has felt his presence before," Daniel answers. "Do you know any Minders?"

"Not ones who would dare speak openly about their Gifts," Jelan answers.

"How could a Minder help?" inquires Akuna.

"Let me speak with a friend," says Daniel. "He may not have the skill required to search your mind for the knowledge, but I'm certain he will know how to find somebody. Do I have your permission to proceed? It will mean sharing the contract details with him or one of his colleagues, but I have worked with him many times before. You can trust him."

Jelan and Akuna clasp hands, silently holding an entire conversation with a few glances.

"Please contact your friend," says Jelan, after a lengthy pause.

Getting up, Daniel faces the wall, closes his eyes, and reaches out to Marcus. A pang of sadness stabs him. He knows exactly who could have reached in and plucked the right information from Akuna Balewa.

Gabriella.

Not wishing to cause Marcus pain, Daniel hesitates before launching a second call. Since he's not a Minder, the best he can do is let it be known he would like to be contacted. Marcus once described it as mental shouting and waving. During the years they worked together, his friend would answer instantly, but these days he has a lot more responsibility. When a few minutes pass without any response, Daniel apologizes, explains the situation, and tells them he will continue trying.

Jelan and Akuna retire to the couch to wait.

Desperate, Daniel calls to Navina Christol. To his surprise, she answers right away.

What can I do for you, Master Daniel?

Instead of answering with words, Daniel opens his mind and sketches the situation with images.

Can you reach Marcus and ask him if he knows who can help?

I can do what you're asking, but not from here. Where are you?

Can't you do a Vision Cast from your location?

This is not a Vision Cast. It's a Thought Transfer. A Vision Cast takes events from one mind or event and projects them onto a visible plane for an audience. A Thought Transfer moves specific

experiences from one person to another. That is what you need to find the exact location of the kidnapping.

Let me explain this to them.

If they are near you and willing to hear from me, I can explain as I did for you.

Daniel conveys the message.

A stillness falls over the room as Jelan and Akuna communicate directly with Navina.

As he waits, Daniel contemplates the pot of tea on the table, trying to remember Lady Corabelle's reasons for advising against drinking anything provided by a house of discreet transactions. A glass of clear liquid appears in front of Daniel's seat.

He blinks to see if he'd imagined it into place.

We have Conjurers to supply our needs. Lady Corabelle was correct. It's best to avoid food and drink at such establishments. Do you think your companions are hungry or thirsty?

Two more glasses appear before Daniel can answer.

I will be there shortly.

More sadness settles on Daniel as Navina unwittingly echoes words Gabriella sent him when she came to help him find Marina. Despite the passage of time, the feeling of helplessness can be revisited any time.

Resigned to a lengthy wait, Daniel sips at the conjured water and wonders what Vic is doing with Katrina and Tellen.

Hopefully, she's thoroughly bored.

It's well after time for the evening meal. Since he doesn't keep many scrolls with energy orbs around the cabin, they've probably turned in for the night. Daniel made clear that his bed could be used by either guest, but he doubts the distribution caused any problems. If she's willing to use a shifted form, Katrina can be comfortable anywhere, and Tellen has spent many nights out in a forest or a field.

A soft knock sounds at the door and an attendant announces a new guest for the room.

Daniel swings the door open for Navina, shocked at the quick arrival.

Please don't ask how I got here so swiftly. I am here, and there is work to do.

Recovering, Daniel straightens and rushes through introductions, which aren't necessary because Navina has just spoken with each of them.

Navina directs Akuna to lie down on her back across the couch. The lady looks embarrassed but obeys. Next, Navina has Daniel and Jelan move the three chairs together in front of the couch. They shove the table closer to the door to create enough space for the chairs. Soon, Daniel takes a similar position on his back, lying across the chairs with his head facing the same direction as Akuna's head.

"Close your eyes to minimize distractions," says Navina, placing her right hand on Akuna's forehead and her left hand on Daniel's forehead.

As Daniel wonders how long the process will take, pictures flood his mind. At first, they're random, scattered images of a young boy skipping ahead down the street, colorful fruit stalls in the market, and a beautiful sky full of fluffy white clouds. More images speed by before Daniel can sort and categorize them.

His left hand feels warm, like somebody's holding it. The boy beams up at him.

The child's expression flips to horror. He opens his mouth to scream but hands seize him and pull him away. Terror fills Daniel, then cuts off suddenly.

He feels nothing.

Everything goes dark.

When light returns, he sees the world from a different angle. The white clouds float by above him. A woman's face appears. She looks concerned. She speaks, but Daniel hears only a strange ringing in his ears.

Blank space returns to Daniel's mind.

Wait a moment. I'm going to work with them to map the city of Urdik so I can give you that knowledge. Otherwise, Akuna's information will mean little to you.

Daniel waits for another influx of mental pictures, but eventually, Navina just removes her hand from his forehead. Initially, Daniel thinks something has gone wrong, but when he thinks about Urdik, he knows exactly where the Balewas live, which direction he would need to take to get to the market visited, and where the City Watch and Homeguard stations are located.

"Catch her," says Daniel, sitting up fast enough to get lightheaded.

Jelan steadies Navina and helps her sit on the chair where Daniel's head was a moment ago.

Swinging his feet to the floor, Daniel twists around and gently picks up Navina's left hand.

"I know that was difficult," he says. "Thank you."

"Find the child," Navina orders.

"I intend to," Daniel says solemnly.

Epilogue:
Fears and Dark Forces

Path to Coldhaven near the home of Daniel and Vic, Karnok Mountains
Same day as the zombie attack (Twelve years and four months after Marina's death)
(Vic is thirteen years old)
I don't want to leave.

Vic glances back at the only home she's ever really known. She knows the feeling is irrational. Yesterday and the day before she would have leapt at the chance to go anywhere but being forced to leave because zombies might attack again is awful. When she considers the terrifying blank space in her mind where the battle ought to be, frustrated tears form.

She trips, but Tellen steadies her, taking a moment to right her pack so she's not off balance.

"Eyes ahead, Vic," he says. "Don't look back."

"What if something happens to the cabin?" Vic argues, straining to see around him to check once more.

"I think that's the least of our worries," says Tellen. "Save your strength for walking and keep an eye out for zombies."

"Do you really think there are more of them?" asks Vic.

"Yes, I do," says Tellen. "Which is why we should stay near the Saroth. We'll be safer together."

"Where are they coming from? What do they want?"

"I'm not certain the undead want anything, Vic." Tellen looks like he wants to say more, but instead, he grips her shoulders and physically spins her around so she's facing down the path.

"You have more to say," Vic accuses, letting her feet move a few more steps. "Might as well say it."

"What's that saying your father has about knowing something at the right time?" asks Tellen.

"I'll 'know something when I need to know it and not a moment before,'" Vic supplies, annoyed at how easily the words return to her.

"That's the one," Tellen says cheerfully. "Right now, our efforts need to be spent getting far away from your cabin."

"Why?" Vic has to work to keep the question at a normal volume when she really wants to whirl, grab Tellen, and make him recount the entire battle.

Tellen falls quiet long enough to make Vic despair of ever getting an answer.

"Because the dead don't raise themselves," he answers at last. "They were sent after you."

"They're likely to rise again and catch up if you two don't hurry," says Katrina.

"I could use a good rematch," Vic says. She makes fists with her gloved hands. "Maybe I'll remember this fight."

"You fought brilliantly," Tellen assures her. "I've never seen anything like that. It was like a higher power fought through you."

"But what did I do?" Vic wonders.

"I have absolutely no idea," answers Tellen. "And as lovely as it was to witness the first time, we should avoid armed confrontations for at least another hour."

Too weary to keep up the discussion, Vic concentrates on the descent for a while. When they reach a more established trail, the footing becomes less treacherous, giving Vic more time to think.

Sunlight winks off the silver bracers, prompting memories about her past. Father wouldn't tell her much about the quest to find the magic bracers, though he has warned that many dangerous people covet their power. He has many names for the silver bracers, but her favorite is the Lady's grace. She doesn't understand what Father means by the name, but it sounds powerful and elegant. Since he rarely tells whole stories, Vic has had to fill in the gaps with assumptions. The bracers and her gray right hand are proof the attack today wasn't her first encounter with zombies. They had almost killed her as a baby and a few years after that.

Why would anybody send zombies after me? Anybody with that kind of power and motivation would be able to send an army of huntsmen or assassins or regular people to do their bidding, but why bother with me? I'm nobody. I'm just a girl from the Karnok Mountains.

These and similar thoughts tumble around in her head when Katrina and Tellen call a halt for the night.

They make camp near a stream. Vic longs to go for a swim, but she settles for a thorough rinse while the others set up the campsite. Since the fire's too small for proper cooking, the evening meal consists of bread, apples, and nuts taken from the cabin stores.

Katrina insists on taking the first watch but changes her mind when it's clear Vic has no intention of sleeping right away.

"Try to sleep," says Katrina. "We have a long way to go."

"I'm not tired." Vic's irritated tone reveals the truth. "I just want answers."

"The questions will be there tomorrow," says Katrina. "Lie down. I'll stay with you until you sleep." She transforms into a dog and bumps Vic's leg with her head. When that fails to move the girl, she gathers part of Vic's dress in her teeth and tugs.

Knowing there's no escape from the attention, Vic finally sits on her blanket beside the fire.

Katrina sits next to her, pressing her warm fur against Vic's side.

The fire dims as Katrina applies her Saroth Gift.

The day's events catch up to Vic. Overwhelmed, she lets her body fall backward until the blanket catches her.

Again, Katrina moves to a position where her dog form can offer comfort.

Instinctively, Vic buries her face in the warm fur, letting the fear wash out of her as tears.

Slipping free, Katrina takes her human form and pulls Vic into a hug.

Embarrassed, Vic tries to stop crying. The resulting frustration from failing at the task leads to more tears. Sniffling, she attempts to break Katrina's hold.

"You can cry," says Katrina. She restores the fire to full brightness. "It's not a weakness. My father says tears like this are a way to shed negative emotions so you can work on a plan. He never explained the plan part, but he's right. If you pretend everything's fine, when it's clearly not, you will only cause yourself more pain. What do you fear?"

When the last tears finally slip out and Vic recovers the ability to speak, she pulls away far enough to look at Katrina's face.

"You're here to protect me, but who protects you and Tellen?" she asks.

Sitting back, Katrina regards Vic as she considers the question.

"Do you know what my father does?"

"Not really," Vic admits.

"He's a spymaster, one of the best in Caramore." Katrina's tone stays even with only a hint of pride. "That means he has many enemies. They could come for him or for me at any moment."

"That's not comforting," Vic points out, wiping the last remnants of tears away.

Katrina grins.

"My point is that many things will always lie beyond your control. Don't worry about them," Katrina advises. "Dark forces would not pursue you if they did not fear you."

"Why would anybody or anything fear me?" Vic demands.

I'm not worth one attempt to kill, let alone three or more.

"I don't know, but you are marked for greatness," says Katrina with a gentle smile. "Try to get some sleep. We can discuss destinies in the morning."

Mention of destinies gives Vic a fluttering feeling in her gut. She tries to imagine what tomorrow and the day after will bring for her, Katrina, and Tellen.

Maybe when we find Father, things will make more sense.

THE END

(The story continues in Redeemer Chronicles.)

Thank You for Reading:

As previously noted, this should not be your first Aeris adventure. *The Dark Man's Wrath* and *The Lady's Grace* possess unsettling endings. If you're tempted to throw the book because of a lack of closure, bear with me a moment. This is the conclusion to a prequel trilogy. It was always meant to pave the path to *Redeemer Chronicles Book 1: Awakening*. If you'd like to end your Aeris adventures here, I'm sorry to see you go, but know that things eventually work out. As with *The Huntsman and the Healer*, you could simply fill in "and they lived happily ever after" and move on with your life. If you want to experience the good, the bad, and the ugly stuff in between, read on. As always, if you enjoyed the story, reviews are much appreciated.

Aeris stories in order: *River's Edge Ransom*, *The Huntsman and the Healer*, *The Dark Man's Wrath*, *The Lady's Grace*, *Awakening*, *The Holy War*, and *Reclaim the Darklands*.

Please visit my website: **www.juliecgilbert.com**. Check out the audiobooks (they have fantastic narrators) or try a paperback.

I would love to connect via email:
devyaschildren@gmail.com

Other Contacts:
www.facebook.com/JulieCGilbert2013
www.instagram.com/juliecgilbert_writer/
https://twitter.com/authorgilbert
www.bookbub.com/authors/julie-c-gilbert